Dr. Morbid's Castle of Blood

Masks

Hayden Thorne

Published by Hayden Thorne, 2021.

DR. MORBID'S CASTLE OF BLOOD

*

Also by Hayden Thorne

Arcana Europa
Guardian Angel
The Flowers of St. Aloysius
Hell-Knights
Children of Hyacinth
The Amaranth Maze
A Murder of Crows

Curiosities
Dollhouse
Automata
Eidolon

Dolores
Ambrose
Echoes in the Glass
A Dirge for St. Monica

Ghosts and Tea
The Ghosts of St. Grimald Priory
Agnes of Haywood Hall

A Most Unearthly Rival
The Haunted Inkwell
The House of Creeping Dolls

Grotesqueries
A Castle for Rowena
The Rusted Lily
Primavera

Masks
Masks: The Original Trilogy
Curse of Arachnaman
Mimi Attacks!
Dr. Morbid's Castle of Blood
The Porcelain Carnival

Standalone
Renfred's Masquerade
Rose and Spindle
Gold in the Clouds
Helleville
Icarus in Flight
Arabesque
Banshee
Wollstone
The Glass Minstrel
Henning
The Twilight Gods
The Book of Lost Princes
The Winter Garden and Other Stories

Desmond and Garrick
The Cecilian Blue-Collar Chronicles

Table of Contents

Chapter 1

Peter's birthday was just around the corner—like a three-week corner. Last time I talked to Althea about birthday celebration plans, my boyfriend's birthday was two months away. I guess I should thank Mimi Gallagher and the Deathtrap Debutantes for eating up the first three weeks (at least) of that two-month span with their whackjob heads-shoved-deep-up-their-millionaire-asses shenanigans.

I said "shenanigans." God, Scanlon Dorsey had already worked his way under my skin down to my deepest innards—the ones that you couldn't locate even with a GPS. He was like a 1950s organic, three-ingredient, white bread type of burrowing mole that also sidelined as a psychic vampire. He made a pretty bad sidekick to boot.

As I was saying, that teeny-tiny detour into supervillain craziness for about three weeks distracted everyone from Peter's birthday celebration, and it took us another week following the thorough ass-kicking that the Debutantes received from my superhero girl buddies to pick ourselves up off the floor, dust ourselves off, and then move forward again. Dazed and confused, yeah, but at least we were moving forward. We were also all in our proper ages again, and I wasn't a bunny. Long story, that.

Then it was another week of humdrum existence in the badlands of Vintage City, with my superhero friends back on the streets, protecting everyone from scum and, judging from the explosion of seriously twisted fanfiction online, providing everyone with tons and tons of masturbatory fantasies. That also included tons and tons of major coronary moments for me, seeing as how Calais—Peter's superhero alter ego—was the most popular source of romantic inspiration for all kinds of Mary Sue fanfics.

Oh, and I shouldn't forget that these fangirls (and boys, I'm sure) had expanded to slash fanfiction, this time pairing up Calais with Magnifiman, of all people, and if these fans really knew the truth, they'd freak out because Calais and Magnifiman were brothers. Then again, I'd heard of fans who were totally into twincest or incest fanfics, so as far as that went, I couldn't do anything but wish the worst form of chronic acne and hemorrhoids on each and every one of them. And the body parts involved in those two should be reversed.

By the time the smoke really, finally cleared, we were only three weeks away from Peter's birthday, and while we already knew that Peter's gazillionaire parents had already planned something special for their son, neither the superheroes nor I had gotten our acts together.

The good thing in all this? I got a job. Yeehaw. This meant that I could afford to buy Peter a gift and not have to grovel at Mom's feet for her money. She still hadn't forgiven me for blowing her hard-earned cash on my handmade journal, pen set, and oil lamp. It didn't matter to her that I was actually using them, but I figured that parents tended to lose sight of reality once money was involved. Mom was also way too addicted to coffee and greasy food, which could account for a lot of things, but you didn't hear that from me.

So! Three weeks before Peter's birthday, I stood behind Mrs. Zhang's steam counter, waving away the spiced-up steam rising up from the Kung Pao Chicken pan and fighting the tears as I tried to put together a customer's order.

"Dang," I said, grimacing and blinking while scooping up the stuff into the container I held. "I think your red peppers just melted the lenses from my glasses, Mrs. Zhang. They don't even act like shields anymore."

Two more seconds of agony, and I was free to walk away from that pan, my face pouring with sweat, my eyes looking like I'd just been caught messing around with someone's fancy booze cabinet. I secured the food container and bagged it with plastic cutlery, napkins, and soy sauce packets, while Mrs. Zhang all but demanded money, firstborn, and soul from the guy who waited for his lunch, drool practically coming out like slimy waterfall.

"Here you go," I said, faking a grin. "Enjoy your lunch!" More like late lunch, seeing as how he was eating at two P.M.

"Thanks, kid. Judging from the way you look, I'm in for a real spicy treat," he said, his sunburned face crinkling when he smiled back.

At least I thought he smiled. It was a little hard to say for sure with all the soot and dirt that covered him. He was one of the construction workers who were busy fixing up (or maybe destroying?) the street a couple of blocks away. He was also a big fan of Mrs. Zhang's takeout place and really, really dug the spicy stuff. What I'd give to have him eat ten gallons of Kung Pao Chicken and then get locked in a closet with Scanlon. My guess would be that a few breaths from this guy would doom Scanlon to a lifetime of toilet experiences, given how sensitive he was to anything stronger than water.

"Uh—yeah. You'll love it." I winced as I swept my bangs aside. They were plastered against my forehead, but at least my eyes stopped watering. I could swear that my glasses' plastic lenses were all distorted and half-melted.

"Of course, he love it!" Mrs. Zhang retorted, giving me a punch on the shoulder. Go, boss. "He always come back for anything that make dead people wake up, eh?" She turned to the customer and nodded, snorting, with meant that she was pleased and flattered.

"Got that right. Keeps everyone else from wanting to sample my lunch. I'll see you guys next time." With a smart salute to Mrs. Zhang, who laughed, he turned around and tromped off, leaving a trail of dirt on the floor. He was like a mature version of Pig Pen from those Snoopy comic strips. And that trail of dirt didn't even come from his shoes. All that stuff was like things that shook off from his clothes, hair, and skin.

I pinched my mouth shut before I got snarky in front of my boss as I turned around to look for the broom and dustpan. "Man," I muttered, walking around the steam counter to the main customer area. "There should be a law requiring people to have a shower and a fresh change of clothes before walking inside any food-serving place."

I grumbled on and on about the grossness of carcinogenic stuff finding its way into a takeout place, which turned into a pretty interesting stream-of-consciousness moment that led me from crap on people's bodies to Peter's naked body, but I was probably just tired.

"Hey," Mrs. Zhang called out, her voice breaking up my sweet, sweet thoughts. "You fantasizing about boyfriend again?"

"Huh?" I glanced back and blinked. "Huh?"

She rolled her eyes and pointed at something behind me. I turned around and saw that I was practically sweeping my way through a wall. I'd reached the dead end, and I never even realized it. I cleared my throat and swept the dirt into the dustpan.

"I was only being thorough," I said. "You should see what's been lurking in the darkest corners of your takeout place, Mrs. Zhang. That one over there's like a portal to the underworld, considering what I'd just swept out of it. Must've been Cerberus' fossilized dog poop."

She narrowed her eyes at me. "You want your paycheck or not?"

That was a shocker. "Seriously?"

Mrs. Zhang shook her head and waved at me. "Come here, come here, and get your money. Now you have something to spend on hot boyfriend, right? Save some for yourself, though!"

I happily dumped the dirt in the garbage can, set aside the broom and dustpan, then trotted off to the rest room to wash my hands, dollar signs dancing in my head. I went to one of the back rooms, where the accounting took place. There I waited while Mrs. Zhang dug around a small safe box type of thing. She pulled out an envelope and handed it over to me.

"Good job," she said, beaming, and she actually looked sincere. "Mom and Dad would be proud of you, newbie." She even leaned close and pinched my cheek.

"Wow, thanks!" I stared at the envelope, which was this plain white one with my name scribbled across it in Chinese characters. At least that would be my name in Chinese, Mrs. Zhang once said, which was really cool. My first paycheck—and no one had a right to touch it but me! Okay, and the freakin' government, but I gotta take the bitter with the sweet.

"Take it to a bank and start saving—well, after you treat Mr. Hot Boy to dinner or something." She paused and glanced at her watch. "Just in time. You clocking out now, right?"

"Oh." I looked at mine. "Yeah, I am. I gotta go with a friend to find something for Peter's birthday." I looked back at her. "By the way, you don't happen to have any ideas on what to give him, do you? He'll be seventeen, he's rich, and he's gay."

Mrs. Zhang stared at me, all blank. "I'm not gay. You are. What would *you* want for your birthday?"

"Sex?"

She stared at me again. "And?"

"Sex?"

She made a vague gesture with her hand. "Is that what teenagers call TMI?"

I shrugged. "Yeah, pretty much. I guess it's also a reason for you to fire me or send me to court for sexual harassment or something like that, so I guess I should stop." I paused to consider something. "You should've seen the look on your face when you heard me, though."

"Oh, just go and find him something nice before you ruin mental image I have of you as crazy, too-skinny boy. I should report this to Mrs. Plath, you know. You be grounded for rest of your life. If she doesn't do it, I will."

I grinned at her and waved as I walked out the door. "You won't. You love me too much. Thanks, Mrs. Zhang! I'll be back on Monday!"

She called something out in Chinese, which I didn't even bother trying to guess, though I was sure she just called me a perv and stuff while sounding really cheerful about it. When I passed the kitchen, I poked my head inside and said goodbye to Mr. Zhang, who was busy putting pots away. He smiled, said something in Chinese, which I guessed to be something way nicer than what his wife said, and waved at me.

I gathered my jacket after stuffing my paycheck in the deepest and most secure zipped pocket of my messenger bag. Then I clocked out and left the take-out place. I was set to meet Wade downtown, and she was going to help me find something to buy for Peter. Apparently she was like me, slacking in the gift department, though I was sure that the rest of the heroes except for Trent—Magnifiman's alter ego and Peter's older brother—were also scrambling for ideas.

It was an easy walk from my job to downtown Vintage. Considering how unlucky this city had been since the superheroes and supervillains came into their powers, one would think that we'd be shopping elsewhere to make sure that we didn't run the risk of getting flattened by falling debris from some explosion or other. Unfortunately, Wade was one of the superheroes, and she couldn't really wander too far because the city needed her. If anything, she was sneaking in some shopping time before she was set to turn into Miss Pyro and watch over everyone along with the rest of the heroes.

I found her sitting on a bench in one of the more froufrou side streets, dressed in a T-shirt, jeans, and boots, her straight, dark hair hanging loose around her shoulders, her massive shoulder bag sitting beside her. She was busy messing around with her phone when I walked up to her.

"What, sending out pornographic text messages again?"

Wade looked up, startled, and then grinned. "Yeah—there's money to be made in this."

"I'm telling your mom." I sat down beside her with a tired but happy sigh. "Hope you weren't waiting too long."

"Nah. I just got here after spending way too much time looking at chocolate." She turned her phone off and dumped it inside her bag.

"Dude, that's totally against Nature. You looked at chocolate and didn't buy any? And you being a girl? What's wrong with you?"

Wade laughed and stood up, yanking me by my jacket sleeve as she heaved that ginormous bag of hers onto her shoulder. "I'm trying to watch my figure, you big douche. Let's go shop for Peter before you make me change my mind about my diet."

I let her haul me off, her hand still gripping my jacket. "Well, that sucks. I was hoping you'd have dark chocolate to share. The richer, the better."

"Feeling horny again, Eric?"

"When am I *not* feeling horny? I'm a normal teenage boy! I'm supposed to think of sex every one-and-a-half seconds or something."

Wade glanced back to give me this look that I couldn't describe other than "God, how do straight girls put up with this crap from their boyfriends?" before turning around to keep her relentless pace through the afternoon weekend shopping crowd. Man, what I'd give to play matchmaker for her.

"I just got my first ever paycheck, and I have to open an account with a bank," I said, beaming with pride. "At least now I have a set amount to go by, which means no high maintenance shopping for Peter. I'm totally middle-class at best."

"Oh. I was going to suggest getting him a sports car." Wade linked arms with me and led me out of the froufrou side of downtown Vintage, and before long we were lost in the "urban" avenue, which was made up of all kinds of indie stores selling modern and hip stuff. Clothes, gadgets, music, whatever—Wade and I not only window-shopped; we attacked every store there was, starting from one end of the street to the other before crossing the road and then working our way down the opposite side.

"Oh, my God, I want this! No, this! No, no, my bad—*this!*" That was pretty much our conversation. By the halfway mark, I realized that we'd found tons of awesome stuff for ourselves but not a single one for Peter. I froze in my tracks, blinking in the sunlight, sort of like what people did when they'd woken up from a pretty crazy dream. All I was missing were my pillow and my recently used, old "bedroom" towel.

"Huh? What just happened?" I looked around for Wade and found her practically plastered against the window of an edgy urban girls' store, arms and legs spread out and clinging to the glass (as if she could do it, anyway), face pressed against it, breaths fogging up the whole thing. Did girls really go crazy when they shopped? Was that the reason why it was fashionable for them to haul around shoulder bags the size of minivans, so they had plenty of room to stuff their newly bought bling in? Dayum.

When I walked up to Wade, stealing glances around me to see if people saw us and thought that I somehow knew her, I heard her muttering to herself. For a moment I thought she was chanting something pagan or what, but it turned out to be "OMGOMGOMGOMGOMG…"

I cleared my throat and tapped her shoulder. She didn't even flinch. "Hey, Wade," I said, looking around again. Nope, no one was watching us. "Come on, quit it. You're scaring the kids."

All that did was to make her press her face and hands against the glass even harder. I didn't want to imagine what kinds of marks she was going to leave by the time I pried her off with a crowbar. "I wants," she said. "I wants, I wants, I wants."

"Wade, you're supposed to be one of the most level-headed people I know. Stop killing my fantasy, and let's go. There's nothing for Peter here." I gave her shirt another tug and then looked up to find one of the shop employees standing near the window inside, gaping at Wade. She was all gothed out and stuff, pretty intimidating to look at, but she stood there, kind of helpless, her jaw hanging low. Then again, it must've been the combined weight of all those rings and studs decorating her lower lip that dragged her jaw down.

Or I could be nice and blame Wade. I wasn't surprised, really. Considering how tough it was to get my friend unstuck from the window, I could only imagine that Wade was literally pasted against it through her sweat, if not sheer will power. Maybe her superpowers made her develop a special set of invisible, super-strong suction cups on her hands and nose.

Little by little, I managed to pull Wade off the glass, grab hold of her arm, and gently lead her away. I could swear that I thought I heard the familiar popping sounds of suction cups. "Okay, let's move on to the next shop, you little creepazoid," I said. "You just terrorized all the goth employees in there." Never would've thought that I'd live to see the day when a rich girl would actually manage that.

"Eric," she breathed once we were out of harm's way. "That was like urban heaven for girls. I gotta go back there and clean the place out. I wanted to buy everything on the rack that was closest to the window."

Seriously high maintenance. "Wade, you're totally not ghetto," I said.

"I can be!"

"No, you can't. Trust me."

The next store we checked out was all about gadgets, which I wasn't really into. Wade and I moved from one table or shelf to another, picking up stuff, yakking on and on about whether or not Peter would like it, and then putting it back down. If that place were a crime scene, we'd both be busted, considering how many fingerprints we left behind. Nothing struck us, anyway, because we both figured that Peter, being a total nerd, would've put something totally badass together like the communication watch he gave me because he was, you know, like a gay teenage Batman when it came to gadgets. Buying something off a shelf wouldn't even come close to what he liked or what he was capable of fully enjoying.

The clerks didn't look too happy with us, either. We took our sweet time to go through their merchandise, and we didn't even buy one. When we walked past the counter, both guys glared at us, and I pulled the old hat trick on them: a dimpled smile.

Well, it kind of worked on one of them, anyway. The cute geeky guy's frown wavered when I slapped him with my magic dimples. He must be gay.

By the time we reached the last store, we were both tired, hungry, and daydreaming about all kinds of bling we desperately wanted. Nothing for Peter, of course. It was like shopping for someone who didn't exist because we couldn't figure out what would work for him. Even Wade, whose girly instincts I depended on, came up short.

She made a face as she rubbed her belly, looking around and scanning the rest of the shoppers around us. "Man, I'm glad he's your boyfriend, not mine," she said. "I'd go nuts if he were."

"How about if I gave him something practical?" I said, rubbing the back of my neck, which was starting to feel stiff from all that craning and bowing and whatever else we did, checking out merchandise from two billion stores.

"Like what?"

"Dunno. My ass. Won't cost me anything but my virginity."

Wade gave me a dull look. "Let's eat. I'm starving," she said, turning around and linking her arm around mine again. I was starving, too, in more ways than one, but I decided that I'd gone way overboard in the TMI department. So I let myself be led down to whatever eating joint Wade was in the mood for, though I secretly hoped it wouldn't be a jumbo hot dog place because I was going to *die* if it were.

Turned out to be Mexican. I ordered a super burrito with the works—you know, the kind that needed to be held up to my mouth with two hands firmly wrapped around it and that I needed to open my mouth *really wide* in order to take a bite. I couldn't help myself.

Chapter 2

Considering the trauma Mom went through during the recent Debutantes attack on Vintage, I figured it was a good thing to show her my paycheck and make her feel proud of me. I was right.

"Oh, my lord, my baby's a working man now!" she pretty much squeed. Yeah, squeed. The way her words came out of her was definitely *not* a squeal. She also glomped me. Yep. Glomped. Had I known that Mom was a total fangirl, I'd have given her the good news from about fifty miles away, yelling through a gigantic über bullhorn.

By the way, when mothers glomp their sons, it goes like this: spread your arms out as wide as possible (try to reach opposite walls with fingertips); make a total batshit crazy face with eyeballs popping out of sockets, mouth wide, wide, *wide* open so that your terrified son's staring at your tonsils; crouch for a second or two for maximum impact and ignore the growing wet spot on terrified son's jeans; jump back up and then forward, closing your arms around half-dead son and crushing him against your chest while screeching in his ear. By the way, listen carefully and make sure that every single rib he was born with breaks in your hold. That'd be, like, the icing on the maternal cake.

Oh, and ignore his garbled screams for his dad.

"I'm so proud of you," Mom kept saying, jumping up and down while she kept her iron embrace. I thought I heard bits of my broken ribs crumble and impale the rest of my organs. "I shouldn't have kept you back before, honey. I wanted you to stay home and stick with schoolwork, but you're proving me wrong."

My face was blue. I couldn't even talk very well at that point, as I was sure that my insides were all shredded from my broken up skeletal system. I think the only part of my skeleton that stayed safe was my skull, but that meant nothing if all I wanted to do at that moment was double over and puke all over Mom.

"Hekksh whohm." That was supposed to be "Thanks, Mom." It was a little hard being coherent when your tongue was hanging out and turning as blue as your face.

Mom finally let me go, and she clapped her hands on each side of my head, forced my head down, and planted a loud kiss on my forehead. I was so dizzy I could barely stand. When she let me go, it was a good thing that she turned around to dig out her favorite coffee mug, so she could celebrate with her new French Roast blend. I stumbled back and plopped down on a chair when she wasn't looking, my paycheck crumpled in my fist.

"You'll have to open up an account," she said. "I'll go with you since you're only sixteen, and they'll need a signature from me."

I nodded, blinking away the fog and waiting for my brain to stop somersaulting. "Okay."

"I'm not sure if a savings or a checking account would be good for you. On one hand—oh, never mind. The bank rep can help us. Now you have to make sure to leave a certain percentage of your paycheck alone, okay? That's the idea behind your opening an account. It's all about learning responsibility early on, and who knows? You might even save enough for your own car if you want or, even better, for college. Isn't that great?"

And so on and so forth. My brain pretty much shut down after that, and I'd no idea what she kept yammering on and on about. For my part, I liked imagining what she was saying to me.

It went something like this: "Save enough money, so you can marry Peter and buy a fabulous house or cabin somewhere in the wilderness, where no one can ever find you even after you die. Over there you'll be surrounded by miles and miles and miles of forests, mountains, and waterfalls—where you and your husband can skinny dip any time as long as you do it at the bottom, not the top, of a waterfall; otherwise, you'd be crossing that great rainbow bridge together before you're even satisfied whether or not you've really, fully consummated your marriage. Oh, and there'll be lots of gorgeous meadows where you can have picnics and hours of uninterrupted sex while deer look on. Then you can learn how to fish and order your groceries and occasional dinner or lunches online, so you won't have to leave the comfort of your home. By the way, your online connection will be the best and most powerful wireless kind, seeing as how you're tucked away in No Man's Paradise. And since Peter's so good with gadgets, he can invent an electric fence that spans leagues around your wilderness, and it'll be smart enough to fry humans who'll try to cross but keep all animals safe. Though you'll need to make sure that delivery trucks won't be affected, or you'll starve to death."

I love you, Mom. Happy face.

"Eric?"

Totally happy face.

"Eric, are you listening to me?"

I blinked and sat up straight. "What?" I looked around in a minor panic and saw that I was still in Mom's kitchen and that I was still single. WTF?

Mom rolled her eyes and blew at the thick pillar of steam coming out of her mug. "I said that I'm off on Monday, and I can take you to the bank after you get out of your tutorials."

"Oh. Okay. Cool. Thanks, Mom." I stood up, walked over to her, and kissed her cheek. "I gotta take a shower and get ready for dinner. It's been a pretty busy day for me."

"Did you find something for Peter?"

I shook my head and shrugged. "No. Wade and I even went through every shop in that urban fashion section on 9th Street and couldn't find anything."

Mom frowned and cocked her head. "Urban? Is that something that Peter's into?"

"Well—gadgets, mostly. But he's always been the jeans and T-shirt kind of guy, and we figured that there might be something new and cool that would work on him, but most of the stuff we saw were too edgy and hip-hop for Peter." I still thought that going the practical route and offering my virtue to him would be the best birthday gift ever, but as always, it wasn't a good suggestion to bring up in front of one's parent. I never got my poor old gay porn anthology back from Mom, in fact. I'd like to think that she at least recycled it somehow. Maybe using the torn-out pages for Christmas wrapper for my presents would be a good way of doing it, but it was also something that parents were universally too fuddy-duddy to consider. Meh.

"Don't worry, honey. You'll figure something out," Mom said, grinning and ruffling my hair.

I thought things over as I bounded up the stairs to my good ol' attic room, and every possibility I could come up with still fell short of my practical gift idea, i.e., my virginity. Hey, I could even argue that it was green and very eco-friendly! I was recycling old towels, which I'd wash myself using fragrance-free detergents that had organic ingredients! Who the hell would say no to that?

Oh. That's right. Peter would. Damn spoil sport.

* * * *

I went online after dinner and decided that it'd be a cool thing to clear my head by destroying cheesy-looking cheap monsters via the usual video game that came free. Of course, now that I was loaded with cash—in check form, anyway—I could always go for a paid account and end up with better games. Unfortunately all those sweet, sweet mental images I made up earlier about me and Peter lost in the wilderness for the rest of our lives kind of kept my feet on the ground, and I decided not to turn my thoughts down that road.

I suppose I could use the cash for more important stuff than video games.

My favorite cheesy online game was "Troll Warrior", where I got to be an awesome troll that went around slaughtering pixies and sparkly fairies, though I left unicorns alone. They were still horses under that totally phallic horn, anyway, and I loved animals. I carried with me a kickass broadsword and a crossbow whose bolts not only penetrated those nasty fairies but also burned their insides slowly, and I'd watch them expand like ticks did when you dumped them on a hot plate before exploding in a tidal wave of nature-themed blood, which also sparkled.

I pretended that those fairies and pixies were all the Mary Sue fanfics involving Calais that had been posted online, which made my battle scenes all the more awesome. If anything, I'd yet to lose to those little buggers. Ha.

Okay, okay, so I told Peter before to ignore fangirls as there was absolutely no way we could stop them from indulging their fantasies. What I didn't tell him was that no one could stop me from indulging *my* fantasies, and that involved utter carnage and blood-soaked revenge on their fanfiction.

It was in the middle of a particularly grisly pixie massacre when an idea struck me, and I toyed around with it while hacking a perky little pixie into two. I might not be good at multi-tasking in the practical sense, but when I was in The Zone of hack-and-slash video gaming, I was totally on.

"Hmm," I muttered, frowning, while idly swinging my sword at the mass of pink-and-gold pixies that flew down to meet me with cutesy little voices and happy colors everywhere. "I guess I can get him a video game. Peter's a geek, and he kicks my ass all the time when we play."

A teal-themed pixie lost its head when my well-aimed bolt shot through its neck. Sparkling teal blood filled the screen as head went one way, and body went the other.

"Die, Diagnosed-With-Cancer-Heroine-Cliché-Romance-Fanfic! Die!" I snarled. Yeah, I could look around for a cool game to get for him. It might not be much compared to what he was bound to receive from his super rich family, but it'd come from me, and that should be good enough, right?

A pixie whose colors were hot pink and sky blue got chopped up by my pocket knife, which was pretty easy to do because the stupid little shit flew too close, and I was, like, "Oh, God, I *hate* hot pink! Eat *this,* Perfect-Vampire-Girl-Next-Door-Cliché-Romance-Fanfic!" Slash, slash, slash, kick. I couldn't help it. A piece of cut-up pixie floated down too slowly after the carnage, and I had to make my troll kick it out of the way. And then crunch it under its massive boot for good measure.

Man, that game was total therapy for me. By the time I finally came up with a solid gift idea for Peter, my troll had leveled up three times, and an entire island of cutesy pixies and fairies was a wasteland of twitching body parts. I made sure to hop into a boat and sail across the sea till I hit the next island of sparkly sweetness before exiting the game. Oh, I also took care to chop up the boat into a pile of colorful splinters before setting it on fire because the damn thing was a magical size-shifting boat that the stupid fairies built. It was fun watching rainbow-hued smoke rise up, while my troll yelled, shook its fist, and kicked at the pile of burning wood before breaking out in a triumphant dance over the metaphorical slaughter of Calais-centric Mary Sue fanfiction.

The downside, though, is that this was a really easy game. I mean, sure, my troll was swarmed by legions of gross fluff balls, but they never fought back because they were so into being cute and perky and crap. I should find a game where my character could at least be challenged by a pissed off fairy. The resulting slaughter would feel more complete.

The next couple of hours were spent with me scouring the 'net for unusual games that I could buy. I found a few, which I was dying to try out, but I decided to bookmark their pages and then share them with Althea to see what we could do before I spent my hard-earned cash on them.

* * * *

The following day was Sunday, which was always a really "bleah" day for me. My family didn't go to church, being damned-to-eternal-burning heathens, and we usually just kicked back and went our separate ways—or at least Liz did with Scanlon, anyway, while Dad and Mom either puttered around the house or went out for a "parents only" meal or something. I didn't care. I wanted to be left alone and recharge in ways that were completely off-limits to my family. I mean, *really* off-limits. Mr. Happy was very, *very* happy by the time everyone came home.

Monday was Mom's free day, and I was back in the "classroom" with Dr. Dibbs. As usual, he was on time and very efficient with his work. As usual, I did everything I could to delay the inevitable with small talk.

"So how're the heroes coming along with their training?" I asked while pretending to dig around my bag for my books and notes. Too bad I didn't own a magical bag that had a secret portal to an alternate world, where I could "accidentally" lose my school stuff. That way I'd have a legitimate excuse since my family didn't own a dog that I could train to eat my homework. Or at the very least, pee all over it.

"Oh, they're all coming along well, thank you, Mr. Eric." Dr. Dibbs brought in a gigantic mug. He wasn't a big coffee drinker like Mom, but he was Mom's alter ego in the tea department. Every time he carried his mug around, I always saw a couple of those tea bag string thingies with the tea tags attached hanging off the rim. So he liked his tea really potent. "Quickshield, especially, is showing a lot of progress, and he's pretty much caught up with the others. He just needs some fine-tuning to do and a bit of work on his confidence. He still seems shy and a bit confused when placed in a do-or-die situation."

I nodded, still messing around with my bag. "That's good. How about Freddie? Did you put a ban on those inanimate objects masks that he uses sometimes?"

"There is—in a way. Sometimes it's necessary for him to take on that kind of a mask for undercover work."

"No water coolers, though," I said, grimacing. "That was, uh, sort of gross, to be honest."

"Yes, that was going a little too far, I think, but that wasn't Mr. Freddie's fault. The police department happened to tap into his weakness for sugar, and things went haywire. Mr. Eric, are you missing your books or something?" Dr. Dibbs narrowed his eyes at me.

I grinned. "Oh. No, I'm sure they're in here somewhere. Look! I was right! There they are!" Damn. I wanted to draw this one out for as long as I could. All day would've been nice. I sighed as I pulled them out and set them down on my desk. What a stupid hassle school was.

"By the way, the next search-and-rescue practice will be on Friday. We figured that the heroes can go without an extra day of these practice missions, considering how advanced they are now with their powers. We might be keeping a weekly schedule for good, unless something happens that requires a bi-weekly one."

"Cool. Got it."

The universe must've been feeling sorry for me that day, considering what day of the week it was, and it was time to go home before I knew it. Even lunch turned out to be a blur, though I remembered Mom's sandwich, chips, and a bottle of water. I guess my head was too full with thoughts of Peter's gift to pick up on anything else. I ate in the classroom because Brenda's antique shop was swarming with two customers, and I didn't want to get in the way of big sales for her.

Then bim, bam, boom, and I was in the bank with Mom, nearly falling asleep in my chair while the grownups talked on and on about financial responsibility among teenagers and whatever the hell kind of options I had as a newbie bank user. I let Mom figure stuff out for me since I just wanted my money safe but accessible when I needed it the most. Paperwork was filled out, and I was let loose in the world with a brand new savings account and an ATM card. Sweet!

Mom celebrated this rite of passage by treating me to a late afternoon junk food fest at her favorite burger joint. On our way home, I dragged her to one of the nearest game stores to check up on the availability of the games I zeroed in on the previous night. Turned out they had three out of five in stock, which was pretty good.

Mom frowned at the boxes I was examining. "Are these what you want to give Peter for his birthday?"

"Well—they're all options at the moment. I have to do more research on-line to see which one's best." I couldn't help but feel a surge of pride when I said that. Research—wow, how official was that?

Mom pursed her lips as she plucked the boxes from my hands and then read over the product descriptions for, like, twenty minutes apiece. I figured that she was also analyzing all kinds of details or whatnot. Then she looked at me.

"Color me ignorant, honey, but I've always bought into the stereotype of gay kids being a lot less prone to violence than straight kids," she said, narrowing her eyes at me.

"Mom, we're still boys. Being whacked out on hormones goes the same across the board, and that includes the need to massacre monsters." Well, kind of, I guess. If anything, Liz would be more prone to violence than me, being female who was subjected to that monthly torture-everyone-else thing as well as being an older sibling. I wish I could account for the violence levels in Scanlon, but I decided that his method of terrorizing the world because of testosterone meant being this totally creepy 1950's nerd who was lost in the twenty-first century. I guess that was more like mental and psychological violence. You know, like passive-aggression.

"Still! Can't you find something that's less bloody than these?"

"Aw, c'mon, Mom. We're not going to turn into serial killers after playing these things. I play free online games all the time, and I haven't even killed an ant. Unless it was going after my food, which is as good an excuse as any."

Mom's look hardened. "You play free online games? How many and how often?"

Ah, damn. Another bim, bam, boom, and I was under stricter house rules regarding online gaming. So it was like I started out quality time with Mom being the center of her universe and then ended the afternoon being lectured about video games and violence and homework and just about everything else that made a teenager's life meaningful. At least she didn't ground me. I sighed the whole time and nodded and said, "Yes, Mom" or "I'm sorry, Mom" or "You don't love me anymore" and the bazillion variations of those.

The only upside to this was the fact that she felt sorry enough to kiss my cheek before pushing me out of the game store like it was some kind of Hound from Hell that was about to eat me whole. In fact, she'd latched on to my arm with a grip that felt like an iron band and didn't let up till we crossed the threshold of our home. Then she went straight for her coffee mug like it was kind of a magic wand that would get rid of all the bad video game vibes that surrounded me. I wasn't sure, but I thought I heard her mutter weird stuff in Latin or something Harry Potter-ish. It was most likely a special magic spell associated with her French Roast.

I went upstairs to sulk a little before going online to blast some asteroids. Hey, at least the only violence in that game was my ship getting rammed by an asteroid and exploding in space. Man, it looked like I was well on my way to turning into Scanlon Dorsey, Jr. I really should up my gaming ante before I make myself sick from all that wholesome destruction kind of gaming.

Even my Troll Warrior game was starting to freak me out, and I actually spared the lives of a small colony of flower fairies because Mom's lecturing got under my skin. Total suckage, man.

* * * *

"Okay, so what do you think?" I asked, barely keeping myself from jumping up and down in my chair, waiting for Althea to say something. "They're kind of like indie games, I guess, since they were pretty hard to find online. Not everyone knows about them, probably even among diehard gamers."

My computer screen remained black for a moment, and then words appeared in rapid succession—as though someone were typing up a message in hyper speed. But it was just Althea channeling her superhero alter ego, Spirit Wire, doing what she was good at doing: possessing my computer and communicating through text. The results weren't far off from when she'd started coming into her powers months ago. I didn't notice any change in the way my desktop monitor looked; it was still black. I also didn't notice any change in the way the text looked when she "talked" to me; it was still in white against black, though the speed was certainly much, much faster than before. The text also morphed in terms of font. I think now she communicated in 12 pt. Verbatim. Verdant. Whatever. The font name started with a "V," anyway.

They all sound cool. Maybe we can test them out.

I blinked, frowning. "Yeah? Like how? Are you thinking of doing something illegal? Because if you are, I love you."

I'm hardwired not to do that. Try again, you criminal. I was thinking about buying those games and then playing them together, duh!

"Well, that's stupid. The whole point I was trying to make was that I wanted to find out which one was good for me to buy." I must say that it was so boring, being friends with someone who was genetically predisposed to being lawful. "Is there a way for us to, you know, get a hold of the games, test them out discreetly, and then delete them and cover our tracks?"

God, you're hopeless.

"Dude, I'm not rich. I might've just gotten my first paycheck, but it's like minimum wage, and I can't afford to blow it all on stupid games." Seriously, what the hell?

Okay, okay, tell you what. I'll check around in school to see if anyone has those games. Maybe I can borrow them, and we can test them out. Happy?

"Yeah, finally!" I paused, thinking some more. "Hey, how far have you advanced in your powers? Are you able to bring a game alive or something? You know, like, work on a gamer's connection and then turn it into a virtual reality experience? 'Cause that'd be awesome!"

Althea was quiet for a moment. *Hmm. I never thought of that, but I can easily control databases in computer systems. I mean, you've seen how that goes. I'll try the game thing and see what happens.*

"When you have time, though," I cut in. "Can't keep you away from doing all the good guy work, keeping Vintage City free of crime."

It's been slow out there since the Debutantes. I guess people are still recovering from the trauma, and even scumbags are lying low. So, yeah—it's been slow days at the office lately. I must admit, it's kind of creepy.

I beamed. "Cool! We can mess around a little with games till you get called in full time again."

What made you think about game manipulation like that? Are you trying to break into someone's database or something? If you are, I'll have to beat the shit out of you, truss you up like a Thanksgiving turkey, and kick you all the way to the police station.

Ouch. That was what best friends were for, I guess. "Boy, I'll have to make sure that I don't break the law when you're PMS-ing."

Pfft. I'm a girl. Girls are very complex.

"And batshit crazy as all hell, before, during, and after your period," I snapped. "But to answer your question, you psycho, I was wondering if you could somehow get into the game's program or whatever and then tweak it to make it a really kickass experience for Peter when he plays it. You know, like work it so that he's in the game itself, but he doesn't get hurt literally when his character suffers a hit. Or gets totally creamed."

I winced. I just said "creamed." I felt so deprived and miserably virginal.

So basically you want me to screw with something legally made and owned. Yeah. I should beat the shit out of you now, truss you up, and kick you all the way to the police station for saying that.

I rolled my eyes, my brain starting to throb with a dull kind of pain. That usually happened when I hung out with Althea, whether or not she was in person or possessing my computer because she had the superpower, and she was too dang lazy to call me on the phone. "Hey, guess what—you're keeping me from my homework, which makes you an official scumbag in my parents' eyes. I'll see you later, you crazy-ass pile of computer chips."

Ha. You can't deal with justice and truth. And you're as psychotic as I am—only more criminally inclined.

"Well, at least you admit you're psychotic," I said.

Althea was quiet for a moment. *Damn. I didn't see that coming.*

"Score one for the persecuted gay boy," I said. "See you later. And you'd better have those games with you when I do!"

Or what?

I shrugged. "Or I'll get a hold of Grandma Horace and tell her just how much you *love* Bingo Night, and that you can't wait for the next one to come. Oh, and also if she could please get her church to give you a lifetime membership thingie for that because you seriously *love* playing, and you want to do it without your friends, who're nothing more than a distraction when you get down and dirty with those bingo markers. In fact, maybe Grandma Horace can negotiate with the organizers, so they'll make you the official bingo game announcer from now on."

God, when you think like a criminal, you really think like a criminal. I'll catch you later, gutter scum.

I gave her the middle finger, and I think she flipped me off, too, because the monitor exploded in flashing bright white light that lasted for five seconds before dying completely. Maybe she was trying to mimic Pokemon-induced seizures in me. If she were, that was a pathetic way of doing it. I mean, come on. Instead of collapsing on the floor, convulsing and drooling, I just sat at my computer, making a WTF face at it before shaking my head and leaving my room to raid the fridge for a late night snack.

Meh. Althea might have cool superpowers involving computers, but that was total loserville, man. As I put together a peanut butter and jelly sandwich, I tried to think of who to invite for that test game thing I was scheming. Wade played, and so did Ridley and Peter. Wade and Ridley kept a strict schedule, though, and limited their game-playing time because of homework (hello, nerds). Freddie played now and then, but he wasn't too keen on games; besides, being the shapeshifter of the superhero group sort of took care of that. I was sure that masking himself a dozen times in one crime-fighting spree was just like doing a role-playing game, only in real life involving real villains and real danger.

Yeah, I guess I'd have to work my charms on him. Maybe bribe him with sugar the way the cops did during the Debutantes' attacks on Vintage. Or treat him to a cheesy old school Japanese monster film. Or...

Oh, hell, Freddie was a total dork, anyway. He'd say yes to anything that wasn't illegal or gross.

Chapter 3

Talk over breakfast the next morning revolved around Peter's birthday. That'd be the biggest WTF moment of my life. Well, after my stint as The Devil's Trill's tragic sidekick, anyway. It was like living out an episode of *The Twilight Zone* the moment I set foot in the dining room.

"Oh, there you are, honey," Mom said, turning to watch me while she cooked eggs. She even *smiled,* fer chrissakes. "Have you figured out what to get Peter for his birthday yet?"

I slowed my pace as my brain tried to absorb what it was she just said. "Huh?"

"You should take him out for a movie and dinner," Liz piped up from the table. "Sometimes it's best to give someone a night to remember and not physical gifts."

My pace slowed down some more as my head swiveled, so I could make a face at Liz. "Huh?"

"Actually," Dad cut in, raising a fork with a piece of pancake skewered on it. "Major caveat on that 'night to remember' thing that Liz said. Dinner and a movie, Eric. Period. That's as memorable a night as you two boys should have. Know what I mean?"

I stopped completely, staring at Dad now. "Huh?"

"I think it'll be really sweet if you reserve a table that's like in a nice but not posh restaurant," Liz said as she refilled her glass with juice. "Seriously, don't hold back on that. A great meal in a quiet and private corner with a massive bouquet of roses and then a good movie after? Totally romantic."

I inched closer to Mom, who'd turned her attention back to the eggs. Once I was about a foot away, I grabbed hold of the hem of her apron.

"Don't underestimate a quiet walk somewhere. You don't even have to spend so much money to make his birthday memorable. Sometimes the best things are the ones we take for granted all the time," Dad said before wolfing down a piece of bacon.

I tugged at Mom's apron. "Mom," I hissed. "Help me. They're creeping me out."

Mom laughed as she turned off the stove and picked up the platter and its pile of freshly cooked eggs. I kept my hold on her apron as she walked over to the table, and I didn't have a choice but to follow her, still clinging in terror.

"They're only trying to help, honey," she said, giving me a quick kiss. "Now let go of my apron and sit down to eat. You're starting to creep *me* out."

I frowned at everyone before turning around to put together my morning toast and jam. My family must've been chomped alive by giant alien plants, and the people sitting at the table that morning were their body doubles. I wouldn't be surprised if they were created to freak me the hell out till I went crazy and turned heterosexual.

I tried not to listen to them as they all carried on and on about Peter's birthday gift, which was morphing from one thing to another at the rate of two-and-a-half times per second. Suggestions were made about homemade cards. Or fun gift baskets packed with items I'd choose from different stores. Or a shirt with a custom design or phrase (which I was inclined to have "I constantly deprive my loving boyfriend of sex because I was born a sad little killjoy" printed in big, bold letters). Or fun gag gifts that'd make Peter laugh.

I continued to scowl with my back turned to them as I toasted bread and scraped blueberry jam across each slice. After five more minutes of this, I finally realized what was happening and rolled my eyes. Dumping the used butter knife in the sink, I picked up my plate and made my way to the table, shaking my head.

"It's a slow news day, isn't it, Dad?" I said as I plunked myself down on my chair.

Dad sighed, nodding. "It is. Nothing's on the news lately. Even the rest of the world seems to be taking a quick break from destroying itself. It's not normal, and I'm starting to get worried."

"I figured as much." My family was bored out of their minds. No wonder they were all nice to me. "Why don't you cook up trouble, Liz, and get the heroes going? I'm sure they're all just as bored as everyone else. Take Scanlon with you when you get them riled up with something illegal."

Liz turned to Mom. "Told you it won't work, Mom. Being nice to Eric makes him even more obnoxious than he already is. What did you eat while you were pregnant with him? Rat poison?"

"Eric, you really shouldn't be so ungrateful whenever someone tries to help you out," Dad said, frowning at me. He continued to use his fork and whatever piece of food was impaled on it as an extension of his finger, as he moved it like he was shaking his finger at me. You know, the way parents shake their fingers at their kids because they totally misunderstood their own flesh and blood and were pissed off as a result. "Everyone here knows that you're having a hard time finding a gift for your boyfriend. Is it too much to ask to—as you kids say it—get with the program and carry on a conversation with us without whining or bullying your sister?"

"I didn't raise you to be a brat, Eric," Mom said as she held up her steaming mug of morning coffee. Come to think of it, it must've been her second mug for the day.

I sighed happily and sank down in my chair as I gorged on food. Ah, there it was. Back to normal. I also decided not to talk about Peter's birthday because that was my deal, and while I secretly appreciated everyone's suggestions, they were still nowhere near my ultimate perfect gift (yep—my ass), and it was a sore point for me.

"Mom, Dad, you'll have to admit that being nice to me is like tumbling down the rabbit hole. It's unnerving being on the receiving end, considering the abuse I put up with every day. I used to think that running away because everyone picks on me would be good, but I think running away because everyone's so nice and out of character is a lot more logical."

"Yup. Looks like rat poison, all right," Liz said.

* * * *

The walk to "school" only brought home how quiet Vintage City was, and if my family being nice to me was a real freaky, brain-melting moment, sauntering through the streets of Vintage without a single whiff of danger anywhere was like living out a zombie apocalypse movie. I wasn't sure if all the pedestrians I passed were human. I kept a suspicious eye on everyone, hoping I didn't have to resort to using my heavy-ass messenger bag as a weapon or a shield against brain eaters.

In fact, I felt so disoriented that I had to stop next to an old man who was minding his own business, looking through a display window of a cigar shop. I felt happy vibes coming out of him, and I couldn't resist reaching out and giving his arm a jab with my finger. He was caught off-guard and lost his balance, tipping over to his left, and I had to catch him and steady him again.

"Oh, sorry," I said. "I didn't look where I was going. You okay?"

"Eh? Yeah, I'm fine, sonny. Thank you." He nodded and smiled at me, those happy vibes—which kind of wavered and rattled around a bit—coming back in full force. I was tempted to give him another jab just to irritate him and reassure myself that the world wasn't going to explode, but I shoved my hands in my jacket pockets and moved on.

I paused in front of Brenda's antique store, looking around me. "What the hell, people?" I muttered. "We're all supposed to be miserable and screwed up!" I sighed and shook my head. The feeling of zombie apocalypse danger faded when I entered Brenda's shop, but it was quickly replaced by the usual spookiness that came with being surrounded by a bunch of old stuff that was once owned by dead people.

Too bad Peter didn't share my morbid taste in things. Otherwise, I'd have bought him a real human skull or preserved innards or a severed hand that was pickling inside a giant mason jar. Then I wouldn't be giving myself a hernia trying to come up with something special for him.

I spotted Brenda in one corner of her shop, moving things around.

"Hiya," I said, and she glanced back over her shoulder, grinned, and waved. "Hey, is there any way for the Sentries to stir up trouble? It's starting to get kind of boring around here, and my family's starting to treat me nice. There's only so much I can handle without going insane."

"Mm-hmm." Brenda straightened up, brushing her hands against her sweater and jeans as she surveyed her handiwork—which didn't make much of a difference with me because her shop was still cluttered, no matter how she arranged merchandise. "You know what you need, sweetie?"

I almost said "sex", but I'd already become way too TMI to Mrs. Zhang and Wade, and I didn't want to subject another female of the species to my needs and the eternal tragedy that was my fate. "Tea and cookies?" I asked. It was safe enough. Besides, it was also a sneaky way of making Brenda serve me with her usual snack tray before "school".

"Yeah, those, but I'm thinking about a pet."

I blinked as Brenda draped an arm around my shoulders and steered me toward the shop's counter, where I was about to be stuffed with baked goodies. "A pet?"

"Yeah, why not? I know that school and your new part-time job are keeping you busy, but sometimes you also need something else to occupy yourself with unless you're a voracious reader."

I sighed and made a face. "My reading privileges were taken away recently."

I felt Brenda's sidelong glance but didn't meet it. I decided not to elaborate on that any more since it meant telling her about my gay porn anthology fiasco and the tragic ending to that story. I was still in mourning, by the way, but did anyone care about the negative effects that would have on a naturally hormone-driven teenage boy? Nope. I'd read about Buddhist monks setting themselves on fire in protest of something, but that was kind of extreme for me. Maybe shaving all my hair off, wrapping myself in a blanket, and sitting in a corner of the house without talking, eating, or drinking would be a more doable alternative in protesting the unfairness that reeked out of the Plath household.

"As I was saying, taking care of a cat or a dog will be good for you. Especially when, you know, the heroes are up to their ears with work, and you're left alone. Besides, having a pet teaches you responsibility and..."

At the sound of "responsibility," my ears snapped shut, and I let Brenda yak away about caring for a living thing while I sighed quietly and tried to imagine all kinds of really kinky scenarios with Peter. And since Brenda mentioned pets, the first thing that came to mind was "fur". So I decided to include a giant faux fur rug in front of a fireplace and all the things that a couple of horny teenage gay boys could do on that rug.

I'd already seated myself on my assigned bar stool, setting my bag aside, while Brenda went to the back room for our snacks. She continued to talk about pets and being responsible and growing up to be an upright citizen because of those, yadda, yadda, yadda. In the meantime, I'd gotten even way more bored than ever, sighing and drumming my fingers against the counter and growing more and more aware of my raging boner, no thanks to faux fur rugs and never-ending gay sex involving positions that would make Chinese acrobats' brains melt with envy.

I'd have to admit that while it was fun on the whole, being a boy and totally drowning in hormones, it could also be a bitch when one was constantly deprived of satisfaction. When did a boy's hormones settle down, anyway? Eighteen or something? I doubted it. I'd heard of guys going to college and turning into testosterone on two legs, and I was sure that had something to do with sudden freedom from living with their parents.

One thing was sure, though—having a family was enough to turn off the faucet, so to speak. It was like having kids meant de-evolving as a human being because there wasn't any time for sex, and even if there were, raising kids could really suck the vitality out of a couple, and they'd look even more sexually uninviting than ever. I mean, come on—how could one picture his own parents doing the dirty? That's just *wrong*.

I didn't realize that I'd been muttering all these things to myself till Brenda broke through my thoughts, standing at the other side of the counter and eyeing me dubiously. Between us sat a platter of homemade cookies and tea.

"You okay, kiddo?" she asked slowly.

"Yeah. Just thinking."

"That must've been some train of thought. You should've seen the look on your face while you talked to yourself."

"I'm feeling tragic right now," I said, helping myself to a cookie. "That was a few minutes of therapy for myself. And be thankful that I didn't subject you to my grief."

Brenda nodded slowly. "Ah. I think I see what you mean. Yeah, I'm lucky." She took a sip of her tea. "So you're bored, huh?"

"I'm dying."

She shook her head and chuckled, helping herself to a cookie. "It's boring from your end, but slow news days are good things for us in the front lines. I'm sure your friends and Peter are all thanking whatever greater power they believe in, if any, for this unexpected breather."

"Yeah, but that doesn't mean they'll be allowed to take some time off." I sighed for the quadrillionth time and gnawed on a chocolate chip cookie. "And even if they were, aren't they genetically predisposed to keep going out in the streets and patrolling the city? If they were actually paid for doing this, they'd be racking up all those overtime hours—especially Magnifiman."

"Sad but true. Unfortunately life isn't always fair, and no one but those geneticists are to blame." Brenda reached across the counter to give my hand a gentle squeeze while flashing me a goofy little smile. "And I hope you don't feel like you're useless or something because you're not one of them."

I shrugged. "I'm over that—sort of, I guess. It does get pretty lonely being stuck at home, while my friends are out there, right in the middle of things. But I know why they keep nagging me about staying put." Peter did say that I grounded him and kept him sane. I thought that was really sweet. Too bad *he* was in danger of making *me* insane with all that crap about "waiting for the right time" and stuff.

Something buzzed softly, and I felt my left wrist tingle. It was the communicator device that Peter gave me, which I thought was better than a cell phone. Or it was a replacement, anyway, because the original got smashed to a million pieces not too long ago, while I was running for my life from that crazy-ass, zombified Calais fangirl. Another long story, that.

"Someone's calling," I said, turning it on. Brenda waited and diverted herself with our food. I stared at the watch face and saw that it was Peter. Well, duh—of course, it'd be him. He owned my communicator device's partner.

Are you free this afternoon? It's been slow, so I can hang out for a bit before turning into Calais.

And just like that, my boner came back. I brought my wrist closer to my face and talked into my "watch." "I don't work today. I'd love to hang out. Where and when?"

A few seconds later, Peter responded. *At the Jumping Bean at around two-thirty. I want you to meet someone, but she won't be staying with us. She's got other things to do. I asked her to hang around for a bit, so I could introduce you to her.*

"That's cool. See you then."

No schmoopy exchanges that time, which was fine with me. I figured that it'd be a good thing to practice being, you know, adult-like and totally cold toward each other. Then again, I knew that Peter sneaked in those messages on the way to class, so no chance for us to get all Romeo and Julian on each other.

Brenda wore this shit-eating grin when I looked up. "See? Told you a slow news day is a blessing for the heroes. Now you get to spend some quality time with Peter."

"Yeah, but I'm still not getting past first base," I grumbled, stuffing my face with an almond cookie. "It always feels like walking up an escalator that's going down."

She nodded and patted my hand, setting her food aside because the shop's bell on the door rang, signaling a customer. "Get a pet, Eric. I'm telling you." And then Brenda was on the main customer area, greeting and chatting up a middle-aged couple.

* * * *

"School" time went by in a blurry haze. Typical, really. I was slowly learning the cold, hard truth about education—public school, private school, private tutoring, or home-schooling, it was all a major drag in the wash, rinse, repeat sort of way. Even if I were able to convince Mom and Dad to keep the tutorials going till I graduated from high school, it wouldn't have mattered. Brenda's cooking or store-bought treats or even orders for freshly cooked takeout stuff wouldn't save me.

High school sucked big, fat, hairy donkey balls.

I couldn't even remember how I managed to get out and find my way to the Jumping Bean. It was a little hard working my brain like that when it had already committed hara-kiri even before lunch. I even messed around with the idea of asking Mom and Dad if I could transfer back to Renaissance High, like, now, but whatever was left of my brain gave me a big kick up the ass and told me to shut up.

I needed a vacation. I wondered if there was such a thing as Spring Break or whatever the hell break with Dr. Dibbs.

The Jumping Bean was crowded, as usual. Students just out of school flocked there, and so did caffeine-addicted employees from nearby shops and banks. That said, I was surprised to see that Peter and his friend snagged a table toward the back. I spotted Peter first, lost in talk with a girl, as I pushed my way through roasted coffee bean-smelling patrons. When I called out to him, he gave a start and then beamed, waving. And there went my heart, all squishy and softy and fluttery. Sometimes I really grossed myself out with my own extreme levels of sap. It didn't help that Peter had ordered me an iced mocha, and it was waiting for me beside his drink.

"Hey," I said, smiling, as I walked up to the table.

Peter made room for me, sliding up the bench and patting the space next to him. "Eric, I want you meet someone." He paused and gave me a quick peck on the cheek, which shocked me, considering that we were in a public place. I blinked for a moment and then glanced at him, wide-eyed. "This is Trini Alvarez. She's from Renaissance High, too, and she's a junior. Trini, this is Eric."

The table where we sat was the corner table in the back of the coffee shop, and the bench was a short, curved one that looked like a midget, wide-mouthed letter C. Peter sat in the middle, and Trini was on his left. She was Latina—or more like a hipster Latina. She wore her hair boyishly short, but the cut was soft and girlish. She also wore trendy, black plastic glasses kind of like mine. She did the double-layer thing with her t-shirts, which worked well, considering how flimsy the fabric was—probably only cost the manufacturer twenty-five cents to make. What I really dug, though, was her collection of those old-school black rubber bracelets that were trendy back in the 80s. It was like one-fourth of her right arm was covered in those bracelets, with maybe five neon-colored ones thrown in randomly. Too bad I didn't look good wearing those; trust me, I experimented with them when I was fifteen. Some people, whose identities I'd rather not reveal, didn't know what to say other than, "My son's gay, isn't he?"

I'm looking at you, Dad.

Trini watched me while Peter made introductions, all quiet and polite and smiling. Then she stuck her hand out and said, "Nice to meet you, finally, Eric. Peter's been telling me a lot about you."

I shook her hand. "Oh, I doubt that," I said between my teeth as I smiled back. "If he did, you'd be running like hell, not shaking my hand."

Trini laughed—another thing I dug about her. She laughed without caring what she sounded like. No, she didn't laugh like a boy, but she snorted when she laughed. It was like that nerd laugh but way cooler because it was her who was doing it.

"Okay, I won't ask too much, then," she said once she settled down.

"So the reason why I want you guys to meet is that Trini's trying to petition the school to start a Gay-Straight Alliance," Peter said, sounding proud. "And I volunteered to help out."

"Is that right?" I said, looking at Peter and then Trini, surprised. "That sounds cool!" I paused for a moment, not sure how to ask, but I figured, why not? "Are you gay, Trini?"

She shook her head. "No, but my little brother is. He came out to us about a month ago, which was a pretty tough thing for him because Grandpa freaked out, and Dario loves him to pieces." Trini shrugged, but I didn't sense any sadness or anything like that in her. It was like she was simply reporting facts to us. "Grandpa comes from a different world, anyway, so it's kind of understandable that he'd react like that. Mom and Dad are trying to deal with it, but they're not giving Dario hell, at least. Or like, they're still trying to figure out where to go from there, know what I mean? Me and Marta are cool with it. Oh, she's my older sister."

"And you want to start a GSA to help Dario," I said, impressed.

"Yup. He's still going through a rough time at home, and he needs support. The more friends he meets, the better, especially since he identifies as transgender, but he's really not free to, you know, dress up the way he feels. I gotta admit that I don't know much about transgender people, so I'm still learning as I go. And—at the moment he doesn't want anyone to use 'she' or 'her' when talking about him. He said he wants to be comfortable with himself first. I mean—he's gone back and forth about being transgender, you know? This is all too crazy new for him, which makes it even more confusing to me since I'm also pretty new to all of this."

I got it. If Trini and Dario didn't have any support at home and expected a major pushback from their own parents and so on, it only made sense if Dario was kind of hesitant about the pronoun usage.

Peter turned to me. "We're looking for a faculty moderator right now, but it shouldn't be a problem finding one. I mean—there's Mrs. Klein, who teaches Biology, and she's like a flaming liberal. Trini said that Dario came out to her first before everyone else, and she was the one who gave him advice."

"Does she have a gay kid?" I asked, and both Peter and Trini shook their heads. "I hope she makes a good moderator if she takes on the job."

"We just started putting things together, and there's no guarantee that this'll happen," Trini said. "But even if it doesn't, we can at least say that we tried, right?"

I was definitely impressed. "You should get into politics someday," I said. "You can be, like, a straight ally spokesperson for gay rights or something."

Trini grinned and giggled. "Not sure what I really want to do yet, but politics isn't out of the picture. At the moment, when I get upset over shit, I just blast things on my computer. It's loaded with old, cheesy computer games. That's why I take real good care of it. If it dies, there's no way I'm going to be able to get those games again." She paused and leaned forward, dropping her voice to a harsh whisper. "And my parents won't buy us consoles and whatever. They think video games are satanic."

"You own retro games?" I asked, now totally, totally impressed.

"Yeah! Well—it wasn't a choice, anyway. I inherited that computer from a cousin who's nuts. I don't care much how sophisticated a game is. I just like shooting things down and hacking and slashing and stuff. Dario's way better than me." She paused and glanced at her watch. "Oh, I gotta go to work." She slid to the end of the bench and gathered her backpack, which sat next to her. "It's nice to meet you, Eric. We'll have to hang out more often and, you know, chat and stuff. Maybe next time I'll bring Dario with me. I'll see you in school tomorrow, Peter."

I didn't know whether or not Trini was a caffeine junkie, but judging from the way she practically flew past customers, it'd be safe to say yes. Either that or she was just naturally hyper, which might account for her slim figure, which went well with her height. She was even shorter than Wade, and I thought that Wade was the pixiest of all pixies.

I turned to Peter. "Hey, that's pretty cool of you guys to do this. I wish I were in Renaissance still, so I can be a part of that." Actually, that'd be the only reason for my wanting to be back in regular school, anyway.

"You will be, once you're done with your tutorials, right?" Peter looked at me and fell silent for a bit, still smiling. "This is nice."

"Smelling like roasted coffee beans?" I wrinkled my nose, pressed my jacket sleeve against it, and inhaled. I think my clothes totally soaked in the scent of Sumatra Blend after only five minutes of sitting there. "Wow."

"No, I mean just chilling like this, not having to look at my watch all the time because I need to turn into Calais by such-and-such hour and shit." He picked up his drink and sipped, even smacking his lips like a kid, which was a rare sight. Then he giggled—like a girl—looking like he was having way too much fun. I couldn't help but stare at him, totally amused. And horny. Not that *that* was newsworthy, you know, but that lip-smacking thing did it.

"What do you want to do?" I took a few big gulps of my iced mocha, which was a pretty impressive feat, seeing as how I was able to do that with a straw. But I needed to pretend innocence and not be too suggestive with my question.

Pretending innocence while my hormones were on overdrive was a total bitch, by the way.

"I don't know." Peter looked around, slumping against the backrest. "No idea."

He didn't know? *He didn't know?* There I was, practically serving myself up on a massive silver platter, and *he didn't know?* I frowned, mulling things over. Was there such a thing as a menstrual period for boys? If there were, I sure as heck knew what the symptoms were, and they weren't fun. I needed to calm down and be, you know, mature about this.

I took another ginormous sip of my iced mocha. "I want a pet," I said.

Peter stared at me. "You do?"

"Yeah. I figured having one would teach me something special about responsibility and all that crap. You know, to prepare me for old age."

"Trent and I have always wanted one, too, but Dad's allergic to animals—or, like, fur or dander or whatever. Not that it keeps Mom from being a yearly donor to a bunch of animal welfare organizations, of course." Peter grinned, his eyes twinkling.

"You should do that more often."

"What?"

"Talk about rebellion or even be rebellious. You light up whenever you talk about it, and it's like—when you glow and be spontaneously happy like that, I wanna do you. Not that I need a good reason to get down and dirty with my own boyfriend, but when you light up, I get all sappy and hard." I shrugged. "I wonder if this is what people call idiosyncratic or something that sounds like that."

Peter just listened, drinking his coffee, and blushing.

"I want to add that the urge gets even worse when you blush like that. Stop it."

He calmly set his cup down and wiped his mouth with his napkin. "What time do your parents and sister come home today?"

Oh, fuck it.

I slid to the end of the bench, hoisted my bag over my shoulder in one-and-a-half seconds, and literally reached down to grab hold of Peter's jacket collar, so I could hoist him up, wide-eyed and blinking (and still blushing). "Get your damn bag," I said. He did, and I dragged him out of the coffee shop and hightailed it back home, my hand still fused to his jacket collar. Anyone who watched us probably thought that I was about to turn in some juvenile delinquent to the cops or his parents.

I guess the upside to perpetually frustrated teenage boy hormones was the fact that, while going all the way was still a big no-no, hand jobs and never-ending sloppy kisses weren't. After round number three, my bed threatened to sue me for psychological trauma. I guess that was expected since I completely forgot to bring out my old clean towels and use them to protect my bed. But that was also what happened when a boy's natural horniness stayed pent-up for too long. It was like tunnel vision with the tunnel being about two inches wide.

We lay in my bed for a bit, a sweaty, sticky, tangled mess, but totally all afterglow-y. It was nothing but small talk for the rest of the time, with Peter giving out vibes of complete relaxation and relief. I'd ask him how he dealt with his own pent-up horniness, but I figured that his situation was a lot more complicated than mine, and I didn't have enough brain cells left to absorb the details.

I'd have to say that it was nice, just lying there, holding each other and talking about silly, useless stuff. I'm not sure, but I think we even somehow managed to degrade ourselves to icky baby talk for a few moments. If my bed could talk, it'd add that to its charges ("Gross schmoopy baby talk for ten minutes! What the Hell's wrong with kids nowadays?") When Peter finally left to turn into Calais and keep an eye out for trouble, I was so mellow that I didn't recognize myself. In fact, when everyone came home late that afternoon, Mom thought that I was coming down with the flu, and I had to run as fast as I could back to my room before she thought of jamming our old thermometer up my ass because we hadn't replaced the oral one, which Dad accidentally broke.

Chapter 4

The following afternoon found me in the library—more specifically, one of the quiet study rooms that kept outside noise from messing up a person's concentration. Those things were invented for ADD types, I think.

Anyway, I sat at the round table, scrunched up against Althea as we looked over possible video games we could mess with. She brought her laptop, and so did Ridley, who hung around with us. He was a bigger geek than either me or Althea, so we depended on his suggestions.

"I like this one," he said. "I'm really into monster games or haunted house games, but most of them tend to be way too gory for me. I guess I'm just a wuss when it comes to that, which makes me wonder why I'm a superhero in the first place if I can't handle violence well."

"Dude, you're a superhero because your parents went to those crazy geneticists, who screwed you and your parents over," Althea said in a monotone. What a pal!

"Yeah, but still—you'd think that they'd at least do something about my anti-violence genes, right?" Ridley paused, looking up from his laptop and staring at us. "I don't even know if anti-violence is genetic."

"Actually, that makes sense in your case," I said. "You're a defense hero, not like everyone else. Your powers are for protection, not destruction."

Ridley pursed his lips for a moment and then nodded. "Yeah, I guess you're right. Too bad it makes me kind of a sucky authority on video games, though." He grinned.

"I don't care too much for the gory violent stuff, anyway," I said. I said nada about Troll Warrior, by the way. "I know that Peter's the same."

"Okay. Then what do you guys think of this one?" He moved his laptop to show us, and we frowned at the screen.

"Hey, that sounds pretty cool," Althea said. "Wait. Let me check that out on my laptop." A few seconds of keyboard madness later, Althea and I were on the same page as Ridley, and we three were all geeking out over the game.

"Dr. Morbid's Castle of Blood," I said out loud. "Just the name itself is a winner to me. So what's it about?"

We fell silent for a moment as we read through the game description. It looked like the game was a horror twist on familiar fairy tales, which involved some violence. From the game's website, the idea was to follow the course of each fairy tale in order to level up, destroying the characters because they were all mutated monsters and ghouls till we reached the happily-ever-after part. And that one involved ridding the kingdom of demonic forces that had turned all the princesses, princes, dwarves, crazy-ass stepmothers, etc., into man-eating monsters. Of course, destroying those demonic forces didn't mean resurrecting all the characters we destroyed along the way and have them move around in their normal, un-possessed state, but I suppose the game was made for totally cynical kids who plain hated fairy tales and their boring happily-ever-after stories.

I straddled the fence there, but I wasn't going to say no to destroying Cinderella because I couldn't stand her and all the stories that'd ever been written as knockoffs of that dumb fairy tale. Maybe because it hit way too close to home as far as the Plath household was concerned.

I sat back in my chair, thinking. "Hmm. That sounds kind of simplistic. It's like one of those linear hack-and-slash type of games."

Ridley shrugged. "Sounds like it, but maybe we should check out user reviews first and find out what's going on."

The reviews were mixed but mostly positive. I was right when I said that the game sounded too simplistic, but the idea behind it intrigued me. It sounded fun, and it was obscure enough for me to want to mess with it even more. And people could also choose which fairy tale to explore, the game company offering six different ones.

"So do you think you can tweak with the program to make it a more 3-D kind of game, Althea?" I asked after a while.

She glared at me, and I pressed myself against her even more. I even rested my head against hers, which was a little difficult since she was short. The things I did to pretend sweetness. Depending on how badly wired she was when it came to justice, I expected to stay like that for a while, eventually petrifying my neck muscles, just for the sake of getting on her good side.

"Look, I can't mess with a fixed program on a permanent basis," she said after several failed attempts at dislodging me. If anything, I pissed her off further by letting out little puppy whimpers whenever she tried to shake me off.

"Maybe during a game, I can assimilate myself into the system and make the game-playing more authentic, but it's only good for that session. Know what I mean? That's the extent of my computer-possessing powers, you criminal."

I sighed and sat up. Damn.

"Well—why can't you just buy Peter a game and then treat him to something like that every once in a while?" Ridley piped up. "I mean, sure, it's not as good as if it's permanently tweaked the way you want, but at least for those times when you're in the mood for super-enhanced game-playing, it might be worth it. Peter's not a high maintenance kind of guy, anyway. I'm sure that getting a new game for him to play with here and there is enough for him."

I made a face and scooted my chair away from Althea to think things over. "I'll have to consider it," I said after a while, feeling defeated. "It sounds like a good middle ground, yeah, but I'm having a hard time accepting the fact that a permanent tweak isn't a good idea."

"How about testing it out first?" Ridley asked. "You don't even know if a temporary tweak would work."

I looked at him, surprised. "Will you play with me if I do it?"

"It depends. My parents have a pretty strict rule about game-playing."

"I'll do it," Althea said. She sat back with her arms folded over her chest, her face a mask of pure concentration. "I mean, you can't do anything unless I'm there, anyway, but I'm also getting all worked up over possible new abilities that might come out of it. Who knows where this might lead? The video game will be a testing ground, for sure, but whatever I get out of this can be applied to the usual superhero work that we do, right?" She looked at me and grinned, and I rolled my eyes. "And if it works out, maybe I can play with you guys a lot more for practice."

"You know, you're just as hopeless as I am," I grumbled. "I might be predictable when it comes to doing something borderline illegal, but you're no better in the squeaky-clean truth and justice sort of way." At least I was more interesting, I thought. Althea probably knew it but didn't want to admit it. Ha.

"Sticks and stones, bucko," she said.

"I want to play this game now," Ridley cut in, now sounding more hyper than before. He was practically bouncing in his chair. "I don't care if it's simplistic. I just want to blow the head off a mutated Rumplestiltskin—if not totally disembowel the slimy little motherfucker."

So much for being a mellow, tree-hugging, peace-loving, defense superhero hippie.

* * * *

I never thought I'd live to see the day when walking home from the library bored me to tears. The happy-happy vibes up and down Vintage City continued, and it was like a creepy-ass stress-free zone. Seriously, where the hell were the criminals? This was getting really unnerving. The more cynical side of me would compare this to the "calm before the storm" thing.

Too bad I don't have a non-cynical side because if I did, I'd have something to contrast that with. Oh, well. I guess the best way of looking at this would be "world-weariness" or something like that. Whatever it was that made people smarter than everyone else. Yeah, that.

I took my time walking home since I realized that I was still stuck where Peter's gift was concerned. The whole game-tweaking bit was a genius idea, but Althea said that her powers didn't go that far. Pfft. I didn't know how much Mrs. Horace paid to have Althea's genes fixed, but it looked like she was ripped off. Besides, while I'd appreciate Althea's help, I didn't want her there all the time. I guess I wasn't a very good gamer-techie type who could think more critically about enhanced games and stuff.

So it looked like I was back to square one. Again. Frankly, at that point, I didn't know how many times I ended up in square one, but it wasn't a fun experience. I figured that Liz and Dad were right; maybe a simple romantic dinner and a nice time out that lasted way past our curfews was the best thing I could give Peter.

I was too grumpy, tired, and hungry and so took a quick detour and ended up at Dog in a Bun. The fast-food joint had completely settled down and even redecorated after being attacked by Arachnaman a while ago. That was good. I'd hate to see it go just because some stupid, genetically-manipulated bigot hated anyone who wasn't like him. So I bought my usual—jumbo hot dog with catsup only, fried zucchini with ranch dressing, and a soda—and decided to find a quiet spot somewhere away from the downtown area but which was still a pretty safe place for a kid.

Not that I needed to worry about scum attempting to do me in, given the recent vacuum of excitement that was Vintage City's days. Hell, even Dad said that Bambi Bailey was scraping the bottom of the barrel with her news reports. I think last night it was all about feuding mothers of five-year-old beauty contestants. Too bad I didn't see that one.

I found a little open area near the Yee Apartments. It was a teeny little park-like place that was about half a block in size. It had a few worn out benches and a couple of picnic tables and nothing else but grass and five trees (I counted). There were lots of birds, though, flying or perching themselves on empty benches. Some were on the grass, doing what birds normally did when they were on grass. I'd no idea what that was other than scouting for worms or taking a massive crap on something.

I sat down on one bench and ate my afternoon meal, all brooding. I was so lost in my thoughts, in fact, that I didn't realize that I wasn't alone any more till something nudged my elbow.

"Wha..?" I almost jumped out of my skin. When I looked, I saw a cat sitting on the bench and staring at me.

I kind of just looked at it for a moment before tearing off a piece of my hot dog and setting it on a napkin that I carefully pushed in the cat's direction. It stared at me for another second or two and then ate the hot dog after giving it a few suspicious sniffs.

I wasn't a good judge of animal age, but it looked like the cat was the equivalent of a ten-year-old kid. It wasn't a kitten, for sure, but it was still too small and too young-looking to be an adult-*adult*. It was also dirty and dusty, but I didn't care. Since I'd already eaten half of the hot dog, I decided to give away the rest, though I ate the bun because I didn't think that cats were supposed to eat carbs. I tore up the rest of the hot dog and gave it to my new buddy, who ate everything I set down, though it ignored the fried zucchini. I couldn't help that last part; I felt sorry for the poor thing since it looked pretty thin and scruffy. I didn't want to think about how it ended up there, alone, dirty, and hungry, because I didn't want to bum myself out even more after my disappointment with Peter's gift.

Once we were both done eating, I petted it and rubbed its chin. Its gray and white fur felt surprisingly soft and healthy even though it was covered in dirt. For a stray, I thought it acted surprisingly trusting of human strangers. I guess it was a good thing that it kinda-sorta bonded with me and not some unfeeling douchebag with shit for brains.

"I'm glad you enjoyed your meal," I said, smiling. This was really nice and relaxing. "But I gotta go home. Be careful out here, okay?"

The cat just purred and rubbed itself against my hand before jumping off the bench and trotting off. I watched it go, feeling a little weird. I didn't want it to go away and stay abandoned and subjected to cars, psychotic jerks who tortured animals, and the weather. I tried to shake off the feeling as I picked up my bag and then moved off toward home, dumping the paper bag and empty soda cup in a nearby garbage can. It was hard, but eventually I got over it.

I had to pass by Mrs. Zhang's takeout place on my way home, so I decided to swing by and confirm my schedule for the week.

I crossed the street once I reached the corner where it was located, and just as I was about to enter, I heard tires screeching behind me and then a long, loud honking of a car's horn. I hated car horns, by the way. They always made my skin crawl, and if I had fur, it'd all be standing and making me look like some kind of mammal blowfish on crack.

I turned around, frowning to glare at the stupid driver who did it, and I saw an old, worn out car stopped way before the corner, and the driver had poked his head out of the window and was yelling.

"Go on! Cross the street! Go! Shoo!" he yelled, even sticking an arm out to wave it.

My cat buddy was frozen in mid-crossing, staring at the car in what probably was kitty panic. It was like it had never seen a car before and didn't know what to do next.

I quickly abandoned my spot and jogged over to the cat, picking it up and waving at the driver. "I got it," I said, and jogged back to safety. The car sped away behind me.

"Look, you really shouldn't cross the street like that," I said, holding the dusty, scruffy, skinny little thing up and looking straight into its eyes while it hung from my hands like a wilted stuffed toy. It looked back, all alert and curious—like nothing life-threatening had just happened. "You could get yourself killed if you're not careful."

It started to wriggle, raising its hind legs and using them to claw away at my hands, so I put it down and opened my messenger bag, shoving stuff aside to make room. Oddly, the cat didn't leave. It just sat there, watching me, its tail twitching and stuff.

"Mom and Dad will probably kill me for taking you home, but maybe they'll agree to a temporary room and board until we bring you to a shelter and get you all fixed up for adoption," I said. "Obviously, you can't survive out in the open, freezing like that in front of cars and stuff. Don't know if you're even aware of this, but that's not how you do it. You run like hell."

I picked up the cat and set it inside my bag, keeping the main flap open, so it could peek out and breathe. I carefully slung the bag cross-body and kept it against my front, so I could keep an eye on the little bugger, and the cat didn't even panic or cry. It didn't even try to jump out. It continued to shock me, the way it let itself get kidnapped like this without kicking up a major fuss.

I stared at the door to Mrs. Zhang's takeout place. I guess that'd have to wait. I figured that bringing an animal inside would be a major no-no, so I carried on toward home. Along the way, I thought about what Brenda had told me about pets and responsibility and all that crap, and I started toying with the idea of maybe convincing Mom and Dad to let me keep the cat. If it meant not letting it out of my bedroom, that'd be fine with me. I sure wouldn't want Liz to mess with its head with all kinds of crazy girlie things, especially when she was on the rag.

Besides, maybe there was a way of training the cat and turning it into the equivalent of a black belt karate expert in the way it protects itself and kills threats. A ninja cat for a pet would be so *awesome*.

* * * *

"Eric, you do realize that your cat's got fleas after being a stray for so long," Mom said, narrowing her eyes at me. She kept her arms crossed on her chest.

"Then I'll take it to the vet for a cleaning and shots," I said. The cat sat on my lap while I sat on the fourth step of the first flight of the stairs, blocking everyone's way and making sure that I got their attention. So far it was just Mom. "I've got money in the bank. I'm sure it's not that much to get that done."

"You also need to have it fixed."

I shrugged. "Okay."

"And then you've got food and litter sand and all the usual daily maintenance. You got enough cash in the bank for that?"

"Mom, I'm still working. Even if I run out of money, I can borrow a little from you and Dad, and I'll pay you back when my next paycheck comes." I stroked the cat's fur. "And the cat's name is Grimm, and we should start referring to it as 'he' or 'him.'" To prove my point, I picked up Grimm, turned him over, and flashed my mom with kitty balls.

She pursed her lips, kept her eyes narrowed at me, and her arms still crossed on her chest. "I'll have to talk it over with your father," she said after a moment's pause. "Don't worry, we'll give you a decision over dinner."

I grimaced. "That's hardly fair," I said. "Shouldn't he at least see Grimm first and hear my side?"

"Your side's pretty straightforward, honey, but the main concern here involves practical matters like vet bills and food and all that. If we agree to your request, the responsibility's completely on your shoulders. No one else's. We're not picking up after him, we're not feeding him, and we're not taking him to the vet. We can help you, but you'll have to do everything. Understand?"

I sighed, nodding. "Okay, fine. I'll wait. And, yeah, I already know what I'm supposed to do to be a cat dad. I Googled all the stuff while I was waiting for you to come home. I'm not *that* clueless, Mom."

The front door, which was down the hallway directly in front of the stairs, slammed shut. "Wha—is that a cat? We have a pet? Yay!"

Before I knew what was happening, Mom had to step aside before getting run over, and Liz appeared, all wide-eyed and happy, her arms stretched out, and her hands greedily swiping away at Grimm while I held him tightly against my chest.

"Kitty! Kitty! I love cats! Can I carry him? Her? It?"

I never thought I'd live to see the day when my older sister would regress to a five-year-old. Then again, I never thought I'd live to see the day when my dad would literally turn into an adult-talking toddler, and look what happened when the Debutantes decided to run the show last time.

I let Liz take Grimm, who stayed kind of blasé about everything. Considering how loud his purring was—yep, he actually purred the whole time—one would think that he really got off on being the center of attention. Liz squeed and cooed and gave out all kinds of gross noises when she held Grimm. I suppose that'd have to count for the first step in her traumatizing my cat with girlie behavioral things.

"Are we keeping it?"

"Him," I said. "It's a boy."

Liz turned to Mom, all starry-eyed and glowing. Mom stared at her, sending out Weirded Out Mom Vibes. "I just told your brother that your father and I will have to talk it over."

"But me and Eric have never had a pet since we were kids," Liz said. "Well, we almost did, but that poor puppy died, remember? It wouldn't hurt, would it? I mean, cats are pretty independent, anyway, and are also low maintenance. If it were a dog, there'd be a lot more involved in keeping it, right? I wouldn't mind having a dog, though."

"Careful, Liz, he's got fleas," I said when she tried to let Grimm climb over her shoulder and perch himself that way. She giggled like crazy.

"No worries. One of Scanlon's older sisters is a vet tech. I can take him over to Scanlon's and get him washed, and I need to take a shower and do my laundry, anyway."

"Ew. Scanlon needs help washing?" There went my appetite for dinner.

Liz snorted and made a face at me. "I'm talking about the damn cat," she retorted and then turned to Mom again, who watched and listened the whole time, and I could tell that she was starting to waver. "See, Mom? I can take care of the cat's bath right this moment if you'll let me. That'd be one less thing to worry about."

"See?" I piped up. "Even Liz is willing to help out. And I'll be taking care of everything else. Wouldn't that be a sign of maturity from me? I mean, agreeing to share something with Liz?"

Mom shook her head and raised a hand while Liz and I started talking at the same time, arguing our case in loud voices. I barely even noted the sound of the front door being shoved open with force and then being closed with equal force. "Calm down, you two. I said your father and I still have to talk things over. Just because the flea issue's going to be dealt with tonight, it doesn't mean that—"

"Wha—it's a cat! We have a pet! Took us long enough for this!" Dad cried out from the doorway. Before I knew what was happening, Dad appeared next to Mom, all wide-eyed and grinning and still in his hat and coat, his brief case dangling from his hand. "Here, kitty, kitty, kitty!" he cooed, reaching out his free hand and rubbing Grimm's chin while Grimm balanced himself on Liz's shoulder. "Finally—real, live, low-maintenance, and cheap therapy for me." He looked at me and Liz. "You two know that keeping pets means a longer life span and low blood pressure, right?" Then he swept his gaze across, making sure we were all listening to him. "And I've got dibs on the lap cat thing for the first hour after I come home from work. Consider 5:30 to 6:30 blocked off on your daily calendars."

"Wow," I said, stunned. "Dad, had we known how desperate you are for natural therapy, we'd have gone out and adopted a cat or a dog a long time ago." All this time spent wishing we had a pet, so I could sneak off unwanted dinner and feed it to the animal—all this time wasted for no good reason? Oh, right—Mom. Pfft.

Mom looked like aliens had just invaded her household. She stared at Dad (who totally ignored her while cooing) and then Liz and then me, her mouth hanging open and her eyebrows all scrunched up. I took advantage of that moment of complete mental rattling and smiled sweetly at her. I didn't even need to use my dimples. It was like that wall in Jericho collapsing.

"Look, Mom, he wants to be with you," Liz said, still giggling, and she plucked Grimm off her shoulder and dangled him in front of Mom. Dad continued to babble like a drunk baby, this time scratching behind Grimm's ears. I continued to give her my most saccharine smile, and then Grimm let out a tiny little "Meow!"

And—touchdown.

Mom sighed, took Grimm, and made like a linebacker, shoving everyone away and then disappearing in the kitchen. I heard the jangle of her keys, and then she reappeared, Grimm pressed against her chest, her purse dangling from her elbow. She gave us all a nod.

"I'm off to the vet, and it's everyone's fault that I'm doing this," she said. "Liz, come with me, and help me buy food and litter stuff. Eric, order pizza for dinner tonight."

* * * *

As it turned out, leftover human food wasn't a good thing for pets, so I'd still be stuck whenever meatloaf was served. I guess I'd have to be very sneaky and very creative in getting rid of that Log of Pure Evil and not subject Grimm to its major nastiness and reduce his life span in the worst way possible.

Mom and Liz came home afterward, carrying a squeaky-clean Grimm in his brand spankin' new kitty carrier, along with cans of cat food, a litter box, and sand. Apparently Grimm wasn't supposed to eat for the rest of the night because Mom was going to drop him off to the vet the next morning for neutering. Ow. At least he was washed and de-flead.

Dad made good his demands for lap cat time, but at least he finished dinner first before disappearing with Grimm. After eating, I saw him in the living room, his feet propped up, watching TV, and having his lap warmed by a dozing cat. He stroked Grimm's back almost absent-mindedly, and the glazed look of joy he had while watching TV was...

Okay, it was downright freakin' creepy. I guess he was getting his therapy right there, so I shouldn't complain. Maybe—just maybe—I could play the Grimm card right, and my parents wouldn't think about grounding me for the smallest thing. Yep. Time to train that cat to be my most formidable weapon against parental persecution. My dimples needed backup ammo, anyway.

Since I had the only solo bathroom in the house (score!), while Liz and my parents shared the main one, Grimm's litter box and sand had to go to my attic room with me. Besides, there wasn't any room downstairs, since we only had the combo dining-room-kitchen in one place and the living room across the hallway from it. I did feel kind of bad that Grimm would have to run like hell to the third floor to poop and pee, but I figured I should buy a little bed for him to keep upstairs, so he didn't have to wander too far. Then again, if he couldn't hold it in any more, he'd have to go do his thing in Liz's room, and I'd forgive him for not making it all the way to the attic.

Or whatever. I didn't know how cats operated, seeing as how we'd never had one till now, so I guess it was all trial and error for me.

The only thing was that I hoped Grimm wasn't in the habit of watching people whack off because that'd be totally weird and unnerving.

Chapter 5

I never thought I'd live to see the day when the heroes were actually given time off. I mean, literally. With Vintage City's crime rate plunging—for now, anyway, until a supervillain decided to liven things up a bit—the mayor's office and police department had agreed that the regular roster of cops should be able to handle things without the heroes' help. So far the only reported incidents had been an occasional missing person, which Sgt. Bone and his uniformed minions could deal with.

"Thank God for that," Wade said as she dipped her onion rings in catsup. "I was so bored the past week that I spent half the time playing around with nail polish on the rooftop of the Emporium Grande."

"Yeah, I can tell," Peter said, nodding, and Wade grinned, raising a hand and flashing us her multi-colored nails. Each finger had a different nail color—blue for the thumb, hot pink for the index finger, lime green for the middle finger, blood red for the ring finger, and neon orange for the pinkie finger.

If Wade was in tight-tight spandex as Miss Pyro then, I couldn't wrap my brain around the mechanics behind her being able to bring five different bottles of nail polish along with her. Like, where the hell would she store them? Of course, had I been a straight boy, I'd be mulling over this point and giving myself some major, major material for an evening of awesome Mr. Happy time. As a gay boy? I didn't get it.

"How'd you get them to dry so fast, with you wearing gloves and all that?" Ridley asked, frowning.

"Oh, I just used my powers on my nails and blew a really, really, really toned down fire ball. If anything, it was more like a ball of warm, dry air." Wade turned to Althea. "Hey, Althea, if you're interested in a manicure, I can do that for you in, like, record time."

"I wonder if the Sentries would be interested in knowing all the practical applications of our powers," Peter mused.

"As far as I'm concerned, you've got a gazillion and one ways of applying your strength and hyper speed in practical matters," I muttered, leaning against him. I kept my eyes looking straight ahead, but I could feel the heat oozing out of him after I spoke. Revenge is sweet.

"I just terrorized a dude with his computer by talking to him in the middle of his watching porn," Althea said in between sips of her soda. "I'd have left him alone if I didn't recognize him for that homophobic schmuck who works at the same pharmacy as my mom, and he was getting off on lesbian action. I think I might've sent him to the hospital since I got him in the middle of toy play or something. Whatever homophobic guys use to abuse themselves with because they don't have a woman to do it for them."

I grimaced as I stared at my turkey burger. Althea knew how to ruin my afternoon junk food time.

"Me and Freddie watched a marathon of his old, cheesy monster films," Ridley said, all beaming. Beside him, Freddie nodded while stuffing his face with cheese fries. "I think we should check out the Elms Theater and see what cool B-movie they're showing. I have a new addiction now."

Considering how he was the last to join the superhero ranks and started out defensive and shy because of all the crap he'd been putting up with as an overweight kid, it was nice seeing him relax and get along with new friends. He was still a little shy around everyone, but I think all that extra time outside superhero work—playing video games with Wade, hanging out with Freddie—was working its magic on him. He was also still pretty tight-lipped about his family life, but it wasn't anyone's business, anyway, and as long as he wasn't being picked on for his weight, I was fine with being kept in the dark.

"I've been messing around with art," Peter said, shrugging, as he dumped the rest of his fries on his tray. "It's been a while since I last did something like that on my own, and it was awesome."

I gave him a nudge with my elbow. "Don't tell me—Trent is still Magnifiman during all this down time, working out in the gym or upgrading all the computers in your little hideaway at home, so that superhero work will be way more efficient next time you guys are needed."

Peter looked at me, for a moment as though he were offended. Then he shrugged again, this time giving me a loopy little smile. "Yeah, I can't lie my way out of that one. Trent's always in Type A Personality mode, so there's no fun in his break from crime fighting."

"I must admit, I've been tempted to start a petty crime wave just to piss off Magnifiman."

Peter just narrowed his eyes at me.

"Just kidding! Man, this is great," I said, sitting back and looking around. I was surrounded by a group of superheroes in civilian mode, and we were all hanging out at the local burger joint like normal teenagers. And this would have to be the first time ever since they all came into their powers that we'd be chilling and eating while not talking in code or whatever regarding current supervillain mayhem.

I mean, God, we were *talking*-talking! I guess if boredom coming from a quiet city also meant having a group of regular friends to talk to while things lasted that way, I sure as hell wouldn't complain.

"By the way, Eric," Peter said, breaking up my thoughts. "You don't have to buy me a video game for my birthday."

I stared at him, blinking. Then my head whipped around till I was glaring at Althea, who gave me this really bad interpretation of a Cheshire Cat grin because it was totally obvious who was at fault and whose ass was begging to be kicked.

"Althea!"

"Sorry. Damn Peter caught me asking around for that Dr. Morbid video game in school," she said, still faux-grinning. "If it's any comfort, I found a source after a couple of days of bugging people, and he actually lent me the game. Oh, and I met Trini, who also heard me ask around, and she says the game sounds cool."

Ridley rolled his eyes. "It's not like Althea was being subtle about it, either. Anyway, since we're all pretty much free from hero work, maybe we should try out the game with Althea enhancing it."

I went from plain outraged to outraged and confused. "You found someone? Who? I thought you didn't have a social circle in Renaissance High."

"Oh, bite me," Althea snapped. "It's someone from Chemistry—a new kid. I don't know him much, but he seems cool. Well, kind of distant and cold, but he talked to me. His name's Justin O'Keefe. I think Peter knows him…"

"Sort of," Peter replied. "He's in my Computer Technology class. He's not bad—though he did creep me out when he zeroed in on me on his first day there. Like he knew me from somewhere, but I've never met him before."

"You mean he just came up to you and started chatting you up?" I asked, and Peter nodded his head slowly, as though he weren't sure about his answer.

"Pretty much. He was, like, sitting at one end of the lab, and when I went in, I saw that he was watching the door." Peter paused and shrugged, chuckling. "Not sure what to make of that, but it felt like he was waiting specifically for me."

"Yeah, but why? It's not like he threatened you or anything, right?" Althea prodded. "He didn't do that with me. I think he just overheard me talk about the game and ask some people about it."

"No, he didn't threaten me. He was friendly when we talked—a bit distant like you said, but he wasn't rude or intimidating once you get him started. And we talked about the usual stuff, like classes and what to check out around here—even hinted at the GSA that Trini and I are trying to get off the ground. Don't know if he's gay or not, but he seemed a little tentative when he mentioned it in passing. Like he didn't know how to bring up the subject. Anyway, he said he and his family just moved to Vintage City. I guess it's his way of trying to settle into a new school."

I patted his hand, nodding my head in approval. "Good to see that you were nice to him."

"Okay, backtrack. What—what?" Freddie grimaced.

He and Wade looked confused as hell, so I explained my original plan for Peter's birthday gift, occasionally glaring at Althea for really messing stuff up for me. Once I was done, I glanced at Peter, and he looked all loopy.

"All that grief for me?" he said, grinning and coloring. "You didn't have to go through all that, Eric. I really don't want anything for my birthday. Hanging out with my family and then with you guys and then just Eric is plenty. But..." He reached down and covered my left hand, which rested on my lap, and gave it a tight squeeze. "Thank you. That's really sweet."

I eyed him shiftily. "Then would you be okay with my second choice for a birthday gift?"

"Sure! Why shouldn't—oh."

Peter got it. Blushing again, he gave my hand another squeeze and turned his attention back to his burger, pointedly ignoring everyone else's stares as they all watched him, waiting for his answer. Me? I was so smug and smirking while nibbling away at a piece of fried zucchini.

"Hey, this burger tastes fantastic," he said. "They must've upgraded their seasonings." He tried to sound all chipper and hyper, but his voice came out in a weak little whimper instead. Almost like he never hit puberty at all, and his voice went all over the place.

"Watch and learn, ladies and gentlemen," Freddie piped up. "This is what awaits you when you get involved with a boyfriend or a girlfriend. I've been taking notes from the get-go. I think I'll be single for the rest of my life."

"Me, too," Althea said. "I'm scared now."

Pfft. Straight people. They have no concept of excitement.

By the end of our nice little burger bonding time, we'd all agreed to test out the video game that Althea borrowed, with the thought that it was going to be great practice for her superpowers and maybe even lead to the discovery of a new skill that she could use for crime fighting. Unfortunately, we didn't have a place to go to. My bedroom was out, considering how tiny it was and how ancient my poor old desktop was. Everyone else's places were pretty much out as well for a bunch of different reasons, like parental wrath and unmade bedrooms with curious little secrets.

Then everyone started dropping Dr. Dibbs' name and was looking at me to get on his good side, so we could use my "classroom" for playing video games. Hell, why not, right?

Too bad it was like trying to talk about flowers and free love to an over-educated and very scientific brick wall. That turned out to be my agenda the following morning, being Friday, and no sign of superhero search-and-rescue practice missions in sight.

"But it's for the greater good!" I said. "I mean, think of it this way—Spirit Wire gets to practice her skills in computer manipulation, and she can not only expand on them, but also find a new skill or power she might not have expected. Wouldn't that be great? I mean, think of how it's going to benefit the superheroes in the long run!"

Dr. Dibbs just frowned at me through his glasses while leaning on his elbows and clasping his hands in front of him. He said nothing.

"Please?"

I didn't play the dimple card with him. I'd tried before; it never worked. At least it never worked when it came to manipulating him into not slapping me with Chemistry and Geometry tests. He continued to frown at me and stay quiet. It was freaky as hell. The longer he did it, the more I was tempted to confess to all kinds of sins that I never even committed.

"I'll show you Grimm and let you pet him."

Dr. Dibbs blinked. "Mr. Eric, I'm not one for sexual solicitation from a minor."

"Huh—no! Grimm's my new cat!" I spluttered, grimacing. "Gross! Oh, that's so wrong!"

He just pursed his lips and waited. I swear I could feel blood oozing out of my pores from that stare. It was something that all adults did to teenagers, I guess, when it came to squeezing information out of them. Or if not, just plain messing around with their minds till they collapsed into a guilt-induced coma, even if they were totally innocent of everything.

I sighed, sagging in my chair. "Okay, we're all bored as hell, considering how quiet it is in the crime world, and we wanted to do something normal and teenager-y, know what I mean?"

"Ah, there you go," Dr. Dibbs said, finally straightening up and pulling out his notes for that day's lessons. He adjusted his glasses and rifled through his stuff. "That wasn't too hard now, was it?"

I scratched my head. "So—is that a yes or a no?"

"Hmm? Well, ask Miss Brenda," he said without looking up. "It's her shop space we're using, after all. It's also her computer or laptop whose programs you'll be running into the ground unless you and your friends bring yours along. Regardless, it's also her electricity bill you'll be sucking up."

"That's a pretty depressing way of putting things."

"I never ran for Miss Congeniality, Mr. Eric. Let's get on with our lessons, shall we?"

* * * *

The good thing was that Brenda agreed, which was all that mattered, considering what Dr. Dibbs said. I did promise to bring Grimm with me sometime to show her, which helped make up her mind. Plus I also made sure to get her a big bouquet of flowers and a box of dark chocolate during my lunch break. Sure, those ate up a bit of my savings, but a bored and desperate teenager's gotta do what he's gotta do, I guess.

"The shop will be open, anyway, and I'll be here to monitor you crazy kids," she'd said, though I could barely hear her with her face deeply buried in her bouquet as she sniffed the flowers. "Bring your own food, though. It's usually busy on Saturdays, and I won't have time to pamper you."

"No, that's cool," I'd told her. "We just need your permission to use the back room. We'll bring our own supplies and stuff, and we promise to clean up completely after we're done."

"No noise, too, okay? I don't want to hear any screaming or crashing furniture or whatever it is teenagers do nowadays to celebrate a kill or to throw a tantrum after getting blasted into oblivion."

I communicated all her terms to everyone after "school", and we spent Friday evening preparing for "game day", which included asking my parents' permission to hang out with friends at the last minute. Thank God for my secret weapon.

"It's only for one day, Mom," I said, watching her as she sat at the dining table, reading her magazine and enjoying some relaxing time after dinner. Everything had been cleaned up and put away, and I'd already finished my homework. Too bad those didn't really mean much when it came to playing video games with friends.

"And who's going to be looking after you?" she asked, practically mumbling her words because she was totally fixated on what she was reading.

"Brenda will. And the room's in her shop, and it's the same room I use for my tutorials."

"Video games, though? I heard those things can run on forever. How long are you guys planning on destroying each other?"

"I don't know. Depends on how the game goes. We've never played it before, and part of it's going to be getting used to it—you know, the controls, the commands, the weapons, storyline, whatever."

Mom just went, "Tsk!" and shook her head. I expected as much. I sighed, pulled Grimm out of my jacket where I'd hidden him, and dangled him close enough to Mom so she could sense his soft, furry, purring warmth. Then like clockwork, Grimm let out his tiny little "Meow!"

Mom didn't even look up. Without skipping a beat, she flipped the page of her magazine and said, "Okay, fine. Call me when you get there." Then she raised a hand and petted Grimm before carrying on with her reading. She never once looked at either of us.

"Good boy, kitty," I whispered, carrying Grimm out of the kitchen. "When the dimples fail, you're on. Got that?" I had to carry him upstairs since he was still recovering from getting his nuts snipped, and I spent the rest of my time reading in bed with Grimm curled up on my back, dozing and twitching. He also snored. I never thought that cats snored, but this one did. For a moment I thought I was letting out farts that sounded like some old guy wheezing, but it was my cat snoring. Crazy.

* * * *

It was like an annual Superhero Convention taking place in Brenda's antique shop the next morning. The only things missing were not only Magnifiman, but also fans in cheesy costumes, brandishing superhero action figures and stuff and creeping out their idols.

Brenda stood outside her shop, smoking and getting ogled by pimply-faced teenage boys who walked past. She totally ignored them, of course, being way older and hot in her usual look—tight sweater, skinny jeans, boots, her reddish-brown hair long and curly and eye-catching, her light blue eyes looking sharp and alert.

I jogged up to her, all smiles and perkiness. "Hey, isn't it a little early for you to smoke?"

She eyed me dully. "My shop's about to be invaded by a bunch of bored, temporarily unemployed teenage superheroes," she said. "I think now's as good a time as any to smoke my lungs into a shriveled pair of black, leathery blobs."

"Oh, you love us. Besides, we promised not to wreck your place."

"I know. But you shouldn't underestimate the power of teenage ADD."

I grinned even more broadly, and dug around my messenger bag. "Teenage ADD means lots of crazy gifts for my favorite Sentry agent." I fished out a box of dark chocolates—Belgian this time. And I believed the label, considering how much money I spent on nine pieces of crummy chocolate. My savings were seriously getting eaten up for the sake of fun. I really should create a budget, but it was too boring and stupid, so I kept putting it off.

Brenda stared at the box and then at me, holding her cigarette up the whole time. Then she dissolved in a fit of giggles, shaking her head and taking the box from me with a quick peck on my cheek. "You're a great hustler, kid," she said.

"I worry for Peter. Now get your ass inside and fire up my laptop. I'll tell everyone you're waiting."

Yeah, she was nice enough to lend me her laptop, which was kind of disappointing in a way because I thought she'd have like porn stashed on the hard drive somewhere, but I found nothing. It looked like a laptop she had on the side—a small and somewhat old one that pretty much had zero programs in it beyond the basics. Damn.

So one by one, the rest of the gang showed up with their laptops, with Ridley treating us to pizza later on.

"I'm so excited," he said, looking all sheepish and embarrassed. "I've never had this many friends before. My parents are in shock right now."

"Wait till we actually spend time with them," Peter replied, grinning, as he entered the room, Freddie in tow. He gave me a quick kiss before getting booted out of my personal space. I might love the bastard, but I had dibs on my usual chair and desk, and I wasn't going to share it with anyone, boyfriend or no.

Now I'm nowhere near being a tech geek, but I thought that in order to play, you needed to have the game installed in your computer, but Althea pretty much bypassed that by using her laptop for the main computer, powering up, and then somehow linking it to everyone else's. She sat at Dr. Dibbs' desk, while everyone else found their little corners, with me all nice and comfy at my desk. Freddie, Ridley, and Peter all sat on the floor on cushions that Brenda provided, and Wade was given a chair and a small table as well.

"Okay, here we go. Whatever you do, don't click on anything till I'm done merging everyone," Althea said. Then she fell silent and started concentrating, her brows knitting as she stared at her laptop screen.

Little by little, the screen started glowing a bright white, which reflected off her face till it about blanketed it, and we couldn't see Althea's features at all—only a white head, the faint outline of her glasses as well as her baby dreads. The glow continued for a moment, and we all let out little sounds of surprise when our own laptop screens suddenly broke out in bright light as well. I had to turn away and pinch my eyes shut because it blinded me, and I could feel warmth coming out, pulsing for several seconds before fading, and the screen slowly went back to normal.

"Whoa, that was awesome," Freddie said from his wall. He glanced up, grinning and pointing at his laptop. What a dork.

"You should come up with a computer mask, dude," I said.

"Ugh, no. I hate to think how things'll be with people using the keyboard. I also don't even want to think what part of my anatomy would turn into a keyboard."

"Let's not go there, man," Peter piped up, staring at Freddie with a weird look on his face. "You gave me enough nightmares when you turned into a water cooler."

"You think you've got it bad? Dr. Dibbs had to play temporary therapist for me for a week."

"Okay, okay, here we go, guys!" Wade cut in, practically squealing.

We all went quiet and stared at our screens. Sure enough, the game had begun, with the usual introduction crap playing, yadda, yadda, yadda. "So-and-so Productions, etc." and all that. I looked up and exchanged excited glances with everyone but Althea, who sat like a statue in front. It was pretty freaky looking at her with her fully integrated like that (or whatever term was used to describe her completely meshing with the computer). The white light had gone down, and it looked like the normal screen brightness reflecting off her face. She was rigid, her expression all blank, and her eyes showed nothing but white behind her glasses. She looked like a corpse, which kind of made my skin crawl, but at the same time, I was in awe of her powers.

When she started talking, only her lips moved. "You're all in," she said. Her voice sounded strange, as though she were talking out of one of those old-fashioned walkie-talkie things. It actually had static in it. "Okay, go ahead and create your characters."

"Are you okay, Althea?" Peter asked.

"Yep. That was too easy. I'd laugh if I could, but I feel like I've just had a bath in cement, and I can't do much but flap my gums."

Chattering like little kids, the rest of us created our characters, sometimes laughing at what we came up with, sometimes whining about the options we were given. I decided to be a ranger type of character, complete with cloak and hood, a mask that covered my nose and mouth, a crossbow for my main weapon, and a pair of long knives for backup.

"Hey, how come I can't see everyone else?" Freddie piped up.

"That's because we haven't started yet," Wade said. "Okay, I'm set."

Everyone else said the same, and Althea finally gave us the signal we'd been dying for. "Right—three seconds, and you're in. Three...two...one...now!"

Our screens pulsed white again, but this time it didn't blind me, which was really strange, but that was Althea's power for ya. My screen let out a cloud of warmth, too, enveloping me and making me feel all snuggly and comfy. The light grew around me till it was like I was completely swallowed up by whiteness and soothing warmth. I even looked around me and saw that I was alone, with everyone else all blocked out, at least by my own little white electronic cloud. My chair was still there, and so were my desk and Brenda's laptop.

From somewhere in the screen, I heard Althea's voice. "I'm about to take you all in. Don't move, don't freak out. And it's...now."

Something shot out of the screen and came at me, nearly making me fall back with a little cry, but I clung to the desk and let it wrap itself around me the way the light did, though in this case, the feeling was tighter and harsher—like a giant hand just shot out of my laptop screen, grabbed hold of me with a firm squeeze, and then pulled me inside in a rush of color and static. I still let out a yell of panic, and I thought I heard the others cry out as well.

"Don't freak out, I said! Jeez, you guys! You're all safe! Don't worry!" Althea said, her voice pretty much filling up my immediate world.

The rushing tunnel of colors and static soon gave way to what I could only describe as a hole at the end of a narrow tunnel. Around me the psychedelic weirdness that sucked me in dispersed, breaking apart and then vanishing in the air, while I pitched forward with a yelp, throwing my hands out as the ground flew up to meet me. I hit a hard surface, my breath getting knocked out of me, and I rolled a few times and then stopped.

"What the hell..?" I panted, lying on my back and staring up, my brain still spinning in my skull, and I swore I could hear it slosh around. Above me was an overcast sky, the clouds all thick and totally gray, and they took on shapes that I'd never seen before. They looked more like torn fabric or whatever—shredded bits of something in a dingy shade. I didn't know if it was night or day, but I expected to be drowned in a sudden downpour.

"Oh, my God, are we in the game?" someone spluttered nearby.

I turned and saw a figure push himself up to a sitting position and rubbing the back of his neck gingerly. I frowned. "Peter? What—why are you Calais?"

Peter glanced up at me, startled, and then looked down, bringing his hands up to stare at them. "Oh," he said. "I'm not my character. Hey, Althea? Uh—there's a bit of a glitch."

I sat up as well and looked myself over. I was in civilian clothes. I gazed around and saw Wade as Miss Pyro, Ridley as Quickshield, and Freddie as—well—he'd somehow taken on one of his masks, which was a miniaturized dragon with sparkly scales all over. It kind of made me think of a kid's dumb cartoon character—only sappier. Freddie-sparkly dragon stood up, looked himself over, and shook his head.

"Man," he groaned. "Of all the—I hate this mask the most."

"What've you been doing?" I asked, staring at him. "Is that one of your practice masks or something? Or are you planning to use it to terrorize a bunch of goth kids?"

"It's a practice mask, of course. God, there ain't no way I'm going to use this piece of crap mask in public!"

"Hey, Althea?" Peter called out again. We'd all finally picked ourselves off the ground this time and were all looking around, totally confused. "Is everything okay? Why are we all in superhero form?"

"I don't know," Althea said, her voice alternately fading and vanishing under static and growing louder and crystal clear. "I never said this was going to be a smooth process."

"Well, since we don't look like our avatars and we've all been de-weaponized because of that, I guess we can use our superpowers in the game," Wade said. She paused, thinking. "Wait a sec. There's something not quite right here." Then she turned, raised a hand with the palm out, and aimed it at the nearest boulder. Her hand slowly glowed as she powered up, and I recognized her arsenal. She was about to shoot a series of fire balls. The glow brightened. Then it died.

We all stood there, watching and waiting. Nothing happened. Wade tried again, and this time, her hand didn't even glow.

"Well, that answers my question," Wade said, turning to us and grimacing while shaking her hands as though she'd just strained her wrists. "We're in superhero form, but we don't have our powers."

"Maybe we need to advance in order to get your powers back," I said, scratching my head. "In my case, I need to find weapons to use as I sure as hell am *not* going to survive against demon princesses like this."

"I don't sense anything strange or off-balance or whatever," Althea said. Her voice continued to struggle against static, it seemed. "It's best to move forward and see what happens unless you guys want out now."

"I must admit it's pretty unnerving, but I guess we can move forward cautiously and be ready to get the hell out if something really dangerous comes up," Peter said, and everyone nodded.

"Okay, I guess just look around you and see if you can find something—like clues or whatever. Anything that'll give you an idea of what you need to do first," Althea said. "We all know how the game's supposed to be played, but you can't earn points and advance without missions."

We moved around, taking care to stay within hearing distance of each other. We all ended up in what looked like a woodsy area—more like a forest clearing or something. There were trees that looked generic, and the ground was all covered in rich, thick grass. The land itself was this gentle, rolling kind, and past a small grove of those generic trees, I spotted a tiny cottage with a run-down wooden fence surrounding it several feet away, standing in what looked like a small meadow.

Our surroundings were definitely fake. I mean, everything around us looked like images in a movie screen, and we were all wearing 3-D glasses, so that there was something like depth and stuff. But every blade of grass or leaf on a tree totally looked phony in that CGI kind of way. The textures and colors were exaggerated. When I touched them, though, they felt real and very cold to the touch—like abnormally cold, considering how moderate the temperature was where we were. It was quiet around us, too, but I could hear fake birds chirping from all over, which gave the place a fake-authentic feel. It was really, really weird but cool.

"Hey, guys, over here," I called out, waving at them. "There's a cottage past those trees. Maybe we can talk to someone—or a character."

Everyone walked over to me, but they moved slowly and carefully, as though they were all listening for something. Even Freddie-sparkly-dragon did it, frowning and moving his head side to side. Ridley stopped a couple of times, bowing his head and frowning as well, obviously straining to hear something.

Along the way, the heroes exchanged confused looks that unnerved me. I felt my skin crawl. I knew that superheroes had heightened senses, and they looked to be untouched by their weird transformation in this game. I could hear nothing but the birds, and seeing my friends all tense and cautious from out of the blue creeped me out.

"Um—is something wrong, guys?" I asked as they neared me.

"Not sure," Peter said, frowning. He and the others stopped a few feet away from me, looking around. "I feel weird. Like there's something here, but I can't sense anything else. I mean—there's something, and yet there isn't. It's hard to describe."

"Maybe it's because of the game," I said, shrugging. "It's pretty bizarre being here to begin with. I feel a little off right now, but not enough to be worried about stuff."

"We just need to be extra careful," Wade said. "Let's go check out that cottage."

We turned and started walking through the trees, falling quiet as we did. The heroes' reactions to our environment continued to work themselves under my skin, and it didn't take long for me to get all fidgety and nervous, glancing back and scanning the trees for signs of danger. I saw nothing, though.

The little meadow where the cottage stood looked like something you'd find in a fantasy art book or calendar. Kind of kitschy but visually awesome; then again, I was seeing everything close up because I was actually inside the game, not just a player. This thought sank in, pushing aside my earlier nervousness, and I followed the others as they made their way to the cottage.

"It looks so damn tiny," Freddie said as he stood outside, looking the cottage over. Any little kid would expect him to burn the cottage down with sparkly fire, but he didn't do that, which was too bad. I'd gotten used to his bizarre mask and would've given my kidneys to watch him do exactly that.

"Okay, I'll go in and check it out," Ridley said, trotting over to the door, which was open. Without waiting for anyone else, he entered, and close at his heels was Wade.

Peter, Freddie, and I waited outside, alternately chatting and scanning the general area. From inside the cottage, we could hear voices, with Wade and Ridley talking loudly and excitedly as they explored. It looked like they'd also gotten over their initial weirdness and were getting into the game.

"Guys, there's no one in here," Wade called out after a few moments.

"Keep checking for clues!" Peter yelled back. I decided to walk a short distance from him and Freddie because I wanted to check out the area closed in by the run-down fence. Nothing looked strange. The same thick, fluffy grass covered the ground. I found a few scattered farming tools like a hoe and a rake. A quick glance at the trees marking the edge of the forest showed nothing, and the birds continued to chirp.

"Hey, I found a chest," Ridley answered, his voice a little more muffled than Wade's. "I'm opening it. I'm sure it has something inside."

About a couple of seconds after he said that, I felt the ground under me shift, and along with it came a sound that was like a hiss and a groan. Something wrapped itself around both my knees, and I looked down to find a rotting corpse—a zombie—pushing its way out of the ground, its tattered hands gripping my knees. I yelled and tried to pull myself back somehow, but it kept its hold, and I realized that it wasn't trying to get out of the ground. It was trying to drag me under with it.

The grass under me melted, and so did the soil and whatever else around it. I felt myself sink, dragged down by a corpse.

"Peter! Peter!" I cried, throwing my arms out and scrabbling at the grass. Around me, I heard the others yell, their voices mingling with more hisses and groans. More zombies were pushing their way up through the ground and ambushing the group.

Chapter 6

Okay, so how did one battle a CGI zombie without any weapons? It was only computer animated, so it wasn't a physical threat, anyway, though I didn't care for the idea of being buried alive, CGI or no. I wanted to advance and gain points! So I started kicking and squirming, my fingers raking through the grass as I got dragged farther down.

The grass felt really plastic-y and slippery, and it was damned hard trying to get a solid grip. I kept scrabbling and struggling, sweat drenching my shirt. That thing was surprisingly strong, and I was getting seriously, seriously pissed off.

"Get off me!" I yelled, writhing and twisting and looking more and more like a fish flopping around—with a zombie trying to keep its grip on it. "Ugh! God, you're disgusting!" After this game, I'd have to go to Brenda and commiserate with her regarding zombies and how much we both hated them.

With a groan, the corpse yanked me down with a mighty pull, and I slid farther in till only my hands were on the surface, my fingers stiff and painful and raw from trying to grab at something. As I looked up, I saw the hole created by that thing slowly close around me, and I yelled even more loudly just as my fingers, slippery with sweat, finally lost whatever pathetic grip they had and slipped off.

"Peter!" I screamed.

The hole above me slowly shrank, the gray sky disappearing. Odd, but no loose dirt fell on me. It was like everything was solid and unreal—well, duh—like I was being swallowed up by soft rubber. Just as the hole was about to close, a couple of long and snake-like things shot through, and my wrists were suddenly wrapped with something warm and soft. Whatever those things were stopped me from sinking, and with a strong, steady force, they pulled me back up to the surface.

The corpse that dragged me down lost its hold, and I felt it try to grab me again. I started to kick it harder this time while being pulled up, making sure to keep my legs and feet moving all over the place, so it couldn't get a grip anywhere. I also tried to use the fake earth around me for leverage of sorts, moving my feet against it even though my sneakers slipped constantly, and helping whatever was pulling me out. The earth that surrounded me definitely felt like rubber. It was so bizarre.

After what felt like forever, my head finally popped out of the ground, and I was pulled across the grass. Eventually everything stopped, the things wrapped around my wrists let me go, and I rolled over to my back to take in deep gulps of air while waiting for my head to stop its spinning.

"You okay, dude?"

I opened my eyes and saw something looming above me. It was a ginormous squid staring down at me. Looked like Freddie had managed to transform into his old Kraken mask.

"I'm okay," I said, gasping and waving a tired hand at him. "Thanks. I didn't think I was going to make it there."

"No sweat. Stay here. We got rid of the zombies in this part of the farm. The others are fighting them off elsewhere." Then Freddie Calamari moved away, and it was like total morbid fascination on my part that I watched him hurry off in giant squid form. It was like ballet, the way his tentacles undulated in sequence, propelling his massive body forward. I was alternately amazed and grossed out.

I could hear the others' voices, all yelling and so on. The zombie hissing and groaning grew weaker and weaker, and I figured that they were killing off those bastards one by one. I didn't know exactly what they were doing to get that job done, seeing as how they didn't have their superpowers to begin with, but apparently they were kicking zombie ass. Well, if zombies still had their decomposing asses on them.

Once my brain resettled itself, I rolled myself to my hands and knees and then stumbled to my feet. Blinking away the fog, I looked around and saw a few scattered corpses of *corpses* littering the farm. I braced myself for a moment of extreme vomiting, but nothing came out. I guess the bodies looked like life-sized CGI that they didn't gross me out as much as I'd first expected.

I walked over to one body and stared at it. Yep. It was a zombie, all right. In fact, it was my favorite kind of zombie creature thingie—you know, the kind that only had half a body, with its hips and legs all missing. Those kinds of undead things were cool—mainly because they moved too slowly for them to catch up to you.

They were all deader than dead, but I didn't see any fake blood, which kind of made sense since blood tended to vanish whenever I killed monsters in some of those RPGs I played. In fact, the bodies disappeared once my character walked away from them. I moved off, picking my way past the corpses, and when I paused in front of the cottage and turned around to look back, I saw the area completely devoid of zombies. Like I said, the bodies just disappeared once my character—or in this case, me, myself, and I—moved away from them.

I shook my head. "Wow. This is nuts." But oddly cool, too.

When I turned around again, I spotted something lying on the ground next to a corpse. It gleamed dully in the light, and I recognized it as a sword or a big knife of some kind. A weapon, woohoo! I ran over to it and picked it up, looking it over in amazement.

It felt real, all right. It was weighty enough in my hand but not heavy. I think it was at least twelve inches long, double-edged, and its handle was carved with some pretty cool patterns. Yeah, I could use it, depending on whether or not we were still going to go through with this game.

I realized all of a sudden that the noise had died down, and I turned to find everyone coming back, looking tired but exhilarated. Freddie was still a giant squid, and he followed behind.

"What happened?" I asked, hurrying up to them, bringing the knife with me. "We got ambushed, didn't we?"

"Well—it was one of those usual surprise attacks that're caused by someone picking something valuable up," Ridley said, coloring. "In that case, it was me. I found a scroll in the trunk that I was investigating, and when I picked it up, the zombies came out."

"Hey, Althea," Wade called out, raising a hand to quiet everyone else down. "What's the status so far? We got ambushed, but we're all okay."

Althea's voice continued its fading and crackling. "Nothing so far—I do feel my connection getting stronger, so that's a good thing. Maybe I can try to manipulate a few things here and there and see if that works."

"Hey, don't help us, though! This was pretty fun—weird, but fun!" Wade replied, laughing.

"No worries. I was thinking more along the lines of manipulating the scenery, like move rocks or bring down trees or expand rivers—something like that—without messing up your game. What do you think?"

We all exchanged looks and shrugged. "Sure, why not?" Peter said. "Just stay alert for anything that's even slightly off, and pull us all out at the first sign of danger."

"So you guys still want to continue with this, then?"

"Yeah, sure," Wade said. "Ridley just found our first clue or mission." She turned to Ridley, who was patting his spandex costume for the scroll. "You got it on you?"

He nodded, reaching behind him and pulling it out. I stared, a little weirded out. If superheroes had invisible pockets somewhere in their costumes, that'd be awesome. But they never told me how and where they hid stuff, and it was pretty hard not to let my imagination run wild in the worst way possible.

Peter moved toward me, and my brain latched on to that thought. Maybe he'd let me find out where his secret pockets were later. Happy face.

"So how'd you guys get rid of the monsters?" I asked, frowning at him. He stopped and took the knife I found, holding it up to the sky to stare at it further.

"Fists," he said.

I deflated. "Really? That's it?" Then I spotted Freddie, still in Kraken form. "And tentacle karate or something, I'm sure."

Freddie raised two tentacles and shrugged—or twitched, which was pretty close to a shrug for a creature with no shoulders. I was starting to get hungry for calamari, by the way. "Well, this is only the first battle," he said. "Monsters at this level are easy to beat. You just punch away at them till they lose all their life points and then die."

"Anybody get hurt in the process?" I asked, looking around. Everyone shook their heads. "Seriously? Is it because of the CGI versus real people element in the game? It sure makes sense if it were."

"Nothing's real," Peter replied, handing back the knife to me. "Which puts us at a huge advantage when it comes to battling monsters. I guess this'll turn out to be a way easier game than expected, but it's good for Althea's powers. Hold on to this, Eric."

I grinned at him. "This ain't real, right?"

"Nope, but it is in *this* world, and I guess using it against other real-unreal monsters is better than nothing, even though you won't be hurt by anything that comes after you."

"Okay, lemme try to shift back," Freddie said. "This mask is helpful sometimes, but traveling? God, no." He paused, concentrating. A little flash of light appeared, fizzled, and then reappeared, shining brilliantly this time before disappearing again. Then Freddie shape shifted into his human form without any problems.

"Hey, that means your powers are slowly coming back to you the more you gain points," I said, relieved. "Of course, that also means that I'm totally dead meat with zero abilities and a big knife that makes me feel really badly about my manhood."

Freddie, Wade, and Peter started talking, once in a while testing their powers, and it looked like it was true—the more points they earned in battle, the more powers they got back. For now, it was just super strength for Peter without his hyper speed, and Wade could shoot out fireballs, which were her most basic offense arsenal. Freddie could shape shift, but it looked like he was also limited as to the masks he could wear.

"That's awesome," I said, grinning. "So what about you, Ridley?"

I looked at him, suddenly realizing that he'd fallen silent. While the others continued to talk, he stood apart, reading the scroll, and he looked pale—really pale. Considering that he was a redhead, that'd be like beyond death-white.

"Uh oh," I muttered. "Ridley?"

He glanced up, startled, but still shocked and nervous. At this point, the others had stopped their chatting and had turned to him. "Uh—guys?" he said after swallowing a couple of times. "This game? It's a trap."

"Everyone, I gotta get you all out of there," Althea broke in all of a sudden, her voice sounding urgent and grim. "I just sensed something bad in the program. Are you all there? Don't move—I need to—"

Her words got cut off by loud static, which went on and on and on, sometimes fading, but mostly staying loud and consistent. It was as though the radio reception got severed. Then just as suddenly, that static sound stopped.

"Althea?" Peter called out, frowning. "Hey, Althea? Are you still there? What's happening?"

"Guys," Ridley said, showing us the scroll. "She's gone. We're trapped in here."

Wade plucked the scroll out of his hand and read it out loud. "Hello, losers. Didn't realize it was going to be this easy to trap your pathetic asses and get rid of all of you in one shot. To give you idiots a bit of a heads up—when you pick up the scroll, you get ambushed as a distraction. That buys the program time to slowly cut off your connection to your freak computer friend because, as you probably don't know right now, you're all so incredibly predictable enough to fight against the ambush first before reading what's in the scroll. I wasn't off when I called you losers, right? How funny is that?

"So what's coming to you? Life trapped inside a computer game that'll keep going and going till you all literally get absorbed by it, and you can never get out. It's a race against time, assholes, and you're all going to lose. That's what happens when you fuck around with my family and kick my brother into a high security mental facility. I don't have his abilities, but I've got a little accidental power of my own—mind-reading, which was how I found out who you are without your pathetic, faggy alter egos. This game is a nice little gift big brother and I put together for you through a mental link we made. Oh, yeah, I know how to get you out, but why should I spoil the fun? You'll never catch me, anyway. I'll be gone before you realize what you just got yourselves into.

"Have a good life, jerks. Best regards from Arachnaman and his little brother."

Damn it. Mom and Dad were going to ground me for this.

* * * *

"It's no use, Freddie. She can't hear you. We're completely cut off," Peter said, glancing back over his shoulder to look at Freddie, who'd decided to improvise a new mask. Apparently he was able to do this still, but he couldn't "access" his other already-made masks. I guessed that he had some weird archive somewhere as part of his powers, where he stored all of the masks he created and practiced superhero work in. Or something. For now, he could only make something up on the fly, which wasn't really a good thing for my emotional and mental state.

"I had to try," Freddie said, trotting behind us.

"You sure did," I said. "That's like trying with all guns blazing. Couldn't you have made up a mask that wasn't so—you know—disturbing and gross?"

"I needed all the lung power I could get," Freddie said. He probably rolled his eyes if he had any. He'd decided to improvise a mask that was nothing more than a pair of oversized human lungs connected to a huge mouth, and attached

to the bottom of each lung was a leg and a foot. I mean, I suppose Freddie needed to walk to stay with us, right?

One would've thought that the fact that the lungs' feet were shod in high
tops would've eased the bizarreness of the mask, but it didn't. The whole thing
was still disgusting. Freddie thought that he needed nothing more than a
mouth and lungs in order to holler as loudly and as frequently for Althea,
which, naturally, didn't work. His mask also towered above us at about ten feet
tall—that'd be the best estimate I could make without horfing my breakfast all
over my boyfriend. And when he yelled, he really *yelled*, which said something
about the effectiveness of a mask that was just—yikes. Not only did the rest
of us lose partial hearing whenever he opened his massive yap and hollered for
Althea, random monsters emerged from the shadows to attack us, though I suspected that they came out of their graves or pits or whatever to shut Freddie up.
It was kind of obvious when they slithered out and went straight for him, only
to be ass-whupped by the heroes via some pretty basic levels of super powers.

Unfortunately they wouldn't let me do anything, even when I was armed
with a knife. That bit was very annoying. Maybe they couldn't help themselves
whenever they treated me like a fragile little treasure that needed protecting;
that might've been a built-in feature in their genetic makeup. Still annoying,
though, no matter how I looked at it.

"Dude, you look like something cooked up in a laboratory by a scientist
who's on bad crack," I said, turning back around when I felt a tug on my hand.

Peter was walking a couple of paces ahead, our hands joined, while before
us went Wade and Ridley, who'd just gotten over a massive guilt trip for not
reading the scroll when he got it. It took us upwards of ten or fifteen minutes
of taking turns keeping him from having a breakdown and banging his head
against a tree till he passed out.

"So do we follow the path? That's all we need to do?" Wade asked without
looking back.

"Might as well," Peter said. "I'm sure Althea will get us out of here, but I
think we need to continue with the game till our powers are fully restored, and
we can help her bust our way out of this."

"Agreed," Wade said, giving Ridley a reassuring pat on the back when he
slumped again, his head bowed, his feet dragging, and looking like a really tragic picture of tortured Catholic guilt. Or whatever religion required massive

blows to its followers' conscience till they all collapsed and went crazy or stupid from extreme repression.

I held the knife in my other hand, sometimes raising it to remind myself that I wasn't helpless this time around, even though my friends treated me like some girly princess. I'd definitely kick as much CGI monster ass as I possibly could, earn points and advance (if everyone would freakin' let me!), and pick up better weapons along the way. At that moment, we were walking through a cursed forest that had stray monsters attacking us left and right. They were few and far between, which was cool, but we all pretty much knew that there'd be huge groups of ghouls and whatever lurking out there, waiting for us to show up. At the very least, every dead witch, troll, or werewolf littering the path meant a point or two racked up by us.

Or at least I guessed that we were all amassing points as a group. If we did individually, we'd all be screwed when once the really hard fights came.

"What's-his-face said that there's a way out," Wade mused without breaking her stride.

"We don't need to worry about that," Peter replied. "Once we get a lifeline from outside, we just need to punch a hole in the game and leave—so to speak. Then bust O'Keefe—if that's his real name."

"How do you know it's him?" Ridley asked.

"Who else can it be? He zeroed in on me. He went to Althea with the game, and I seriously doubt if he really overheard her asking anyone about owning one. Like he said, he has mind-reading powers."

I looked at him as we walked side by side. "Do you believe him, though? Do you think he's Arachnaman's brother?"

"Can't say for sure. Althea should get the Sentries and Trent to help and figure out who's what and all that. My only concern right now is for everyone to get out of this."

I heard the sound of hurried footsteps behind, and I dared a look back. Freddie was once again normal, which was a pretty loose word to use when referring to Freddie Jameson. "Yo," he panted, slapping me between the shoulders before overtaking me and Peter and joining Wade and Ridley in the front. Which was ten different shades of awesome, of course, seeing as how my little personal space with Peter wasn't going to be messed with.

I sighed as I trudged onward. This was going to suck. If Mom and Dad were to hear about this little adventure I got myself into, I'd be grounded for an entire lifetime. Maybe two. Or three. If I didn't make it out and became a permanent fixture in the game, it wouldn't matter. They'd take the game home and ground me all the same for being a part of an evil conspiracy to brainwash kids into a lifetime of stupidity and slobbery, knuckle-dragging, monosyllabic grunting. What a life.

I gave Peter's hand a squeeze. "Aren't you glad this isn't your birthday gift?"

He chuckled, returning the pressure. "Was this your original plan?"

"Pretty much. I was hoping to buy you a game, have Althea tweak it for maximum playing enjoyment or whatever the hell it's called, and then give it to you. I mean—you've got everything you need. I wanted to give you something that's unique and specially made for you. Turned out to be a stupid idea. I guess I need to work more on that skill."

"Hey. Come here." He stopped and gave my hand a tug, bringing me close for a kiss that lasted longer than I expected. When he pulled away, he was smiling. "Thank you. Yeah, I've got everything I need. It's right in front of me."

"You're so sappy." And hot. He was in full Calais gear. If he'd let me, I'd climb up his body and fuse myself with him like that, though it'd make us look like incestuous conjoined twins who were connected in the happiest parts of our bodies. I really should write a novel about my experiences. I was sure that a thousand or more other gay boys out there would totally feel my pain, and I could somehow make their lives better by suffering horribly in mine.

"I know I am. Come on. I'm itching to kick monster ass, so I can properly celebrate my birthday with you." Heads up! Peter said "properly".

"Oh, bless you." It was my turn to hurry forward, dragging him behind me. Motivation rocks, people. I, of course, ignored the very real possibility that Peter's definition of "properly" didn't run along the same lines as mine. But being sixteen and sexually frustrated was like mega-sized blinders or whatever you called those things that people put on horses' heads to keep them from getting all distracted and stuff.

In fact, I was so motivated (read: absolutely, positively sexually frustrated) that after five more seconds of walking, I had to shake off Peter's hand and hurry off the road. Nothing was happening to us, and it was starting to piss me off. We needed to earn points and level up! Besides, I was getting so damned bored with the game by now, I wanted to get out and have pizza, and I wanted to do my boyfriend till I passed out from loss of body fluids.

"Eric? What—hey, where are you going?" Peter called.

I didn't bother looking back at him. I had bigger things to worry about. I also tried to ignore Freddie saying, "Oh, great. He's using himself for monster bait. What the hell did you say to him, Peter?"

I held my knife with two hands, raising it in front of me. I mean, yeah, yeah, totally Freudian, but also really, really inspired, know what I mean? "Come on, come on, get your rotting asses out of bed!" I yelled. "I gotta earn myself some points!"

"Peter, *you* fix this." That was Wade, by the way.

"I don't know what I said, I swear!" That was Peter, the big, clueless, lovable dill weed.

"No, no, don't worry!" I called back, glancing behind me and grinning. "I can handle this! The more points we earn, the faster we get out of here!" That ten-second look back yielded some pretty interesting visuals. Like, my super-hero friends all standing in the middle of a forest path, confused and staring at me as though I'd sprouted a dozen penises all over my head and made me look like the porn version of that Pinhead monster thing in those *Hellraiser* movies.

Just off to my right, I heard the rustling of leaves and branches, and I steadied myself. One-to-one combat with, what—another zombie? A witch? A skeleton? A werewolf? Oh, I was ready for it. My friends might have all the kickass abilities and I only had a real-unreal knife, but I wasn't going to lie around, being fed grapes, while everyone else beat the living crap out of monsters to earn the group more and more points. I suppose I also wanted to prove to Peter that I could easily defend myself and everyone else when push came to shove.

Okay, screw it, I desperately wanted those points, so we could bust out of the game, and Peter and I could celebrate his pre-birthday thing the proper way as defined by me. Served him right for planting that idea in my skull.

I was also getting very hungry by then.

The forest really wasn't a forest in the extreme sense. That is, we were surrounded by endless clusters of trees, but there was a lot of space in between them that allowed plenty of artificial sunlight to shine through and help us find our way around. And since it was a video game, the main path that we were following was completely unhindered by shadows and stuff.

"Eric!"

"Let me take care of this and help us earn points! I want to get out of here as much as you do!" Man, Peter could really be a major dud in the excitement department. I mean, seriously.

The rustling quieted down, and a figure emerged from the shadows. Finally! I pinched my mouth into a tight line, furrowing my brows in concentration. Oh, this was going to be great. I could show my genetically altered friends that I could fight my way out of things.

"Gwwaargh..." A low groan that reminded me of those zombies earlier cut through the silence. Cool. I was poised to slaughter the undead. I wished I studied the details of the game before we started because I wanted to know how many points I could rack up, killing something that not only wasn't real, but was also already dead.

A figure appeared, stumbling into the sunlight, its glassy stare fixed on me. "Gwwaargh..." Pinkish drool dangling off its red mouth, the monster came after me, baring its rotting gums. It reeked of death and destruction, and it definitely wanted me for dinner.

Unfortunately it was also about a little over a foot tall, a bald, naked, and disgustingly bloated carcass of—of something that was a little over a foot tall. Its skin was of a bluish-whitish-gray hue that was also riddled with open sores that looked like marks of decay. Was it a zombified baby? It sure as hell looked like it.

I stared at it, drop-jawed, as it teetered over to me and then latched on to my right leg with an undead groan, wrapping its dough-like arms and legs around my shin while fastening its mouth onto my knee. I continued to stare it as it tried to gnaw away at my kneecap, and I lowered my knife.

"Oh, come on," I said, sighing. "What the hell's this crap?" I turned around and pointed at the zombie baby that was fused to my right leg, groaning and chomping my jeans. "How many points does this stupid little thing have?"

"This game has zombie babies?" Wade asked, blinking. The heroes continued to stare at me, confused.

"Apparently," I said, glancing down to shake my head at this little monster thing that was fighting a losing battle against my leg. "Dude, get off. You can't eat me alive if you don't even have any teeth yet. Come on, I don't want to waste my energy cutting you up, when you'll only be earning me, like, one point at most."

"I think it likes you, Eric," Freddie said, frowning.

"I'm not babysitting this thing! Peter, take note—this is what fatherhood is all about. You really want one of these when we finally settle down?" I pointed at the rotting, bloated baby. I guess the great thing about being stuck inside a video game is that the unreality helped during moments like this. That little monster thing kept gnawing away at my leg, but I didn't feel any drool soaking my jeans. If I did, it would've pushed me over the edge, and I'd be feeding the next troll we came across with zombie baby kabobs.

"Not while you and that thing continue your bonding moment like that," Peter said, visibly wincing.

"Dude, are you going to kill it, or not?" Freddie asked. The grimace on his face spoke volumes.

"Gwwaargh...nom...nom...nom...slurp...slobber...nom..."

I sighed, rolling my eyes. "This isn't worth it. So stupid," I grumbled, turning around and hobbling back toward the trees where that toothless thing came from. I glanced down and poked the top of its head with my knife, taking care not to break the skin even though it was totally fake. I wanted to play it safe and make sure that I didn't end up with zombie baby gore all over my jeans. "Come on, kid, get off. I'm sure your undead mom's out there somewhere, looking for you."

"Gwwaargh...nom...nom...slurp..."

"Tsk." I sighed, dropped my knife, and pried the damn thing off, mildly grossed out by the coldness and softness of its arms when I grabbed hold of them and pulled them off my leg. The little monster kept groaning and hissing as it fought against me, trying hard to get itself back on my leg. I held it up and away from me while it kicked and slobbered, its face twisting in what was probably hunger.

"Sorry, man. You're not worth the trouble." I reminded myself one last time that this wasn't real, so I tossed the baby up, waited for it to fall, and then kicked it like a soccer ball at just the right point. It let out a grunt, still growling and hissing as it flew off back into the shadows, a pretty gross-looking bundle of undead flesh tumbling in the air.

I stood for a moment, listening for it to land somewhere, and it eventually did. Slightly muffled sounds of leaves shaking and branches breaking followed, and then came the inevitable thud as the little monster landed. Safely, I suppose. It actually let out a soft "Oof!"

I stooped down to pick up my knife and then trudge back to my friends, who just waited for me. "Well, that was a real disappointment," I said, sulking. "I was hoping to get some fighting experience under my belt, but..." How embarrassing was that? I looked at Peter, frowning. "Do you still want to have kids down the line?"

He looked at me and then past my shoulders, most likely to stare in shock at where I'd just punted that little monster like a pro athlete. "Um...not if that's how you'll be dealing with annoying kiddie behavior."

"Oh, that's how it's going to be, all right," I grumbled as I took his hand and led him away, following the others. "And I was being gentle and forgiving this time."

"Yikes."

"You know, Peter, I have a feeling that I'm going to be a way stricter dad than you."

"Yikes."

Chapter 7

RPG Lesson Number 4,887,302: skeletons were a bitch to kill. About ten minutes after that dumb zombie baby "attack," we were again ambushed by monsters—this time a small group of skeletons. The good news was that I was finally allowed to fight, and it was obvious that the heroes decided that they should feel sorry for me after that pathetic and embarrassing confrontation I had with an undead infant. So I fought alongside my buddies, who were using whatever basic powers they'd earned so far. In their case, they were easily mowing down skeletons.

The bad news for me was that, while I was armed with a knife, it was kind of frustrating swinging away at a flailing skeleton, unable to get points off it because my knife didn't have much to go by but bones, which weren't massive enough to be easy targets. My knife's point kept shooting through those spaces in between ribs, and in those few times when I aimed for the skull, my knife went into an eye socket, which was useless and made me wish that the skeletons walked around with eyeballs that I could stab.

As it was, I had to stop, sighing, and stare at the skeleton that was flailing its arms wildly, trying its best to decrease my life points by injuring me with its bony fingers. Yeah, right—like skeletal appendages scraping my skin actually meant life-threatening injuries and stuff. I didn't even feel any contact from its attacks. It touched me here and there, scratching and clawing, but I felt nothing—no pain whatsoever. It was all like fingers made of soft rubber pawing away at me, and that was it. I even looked down at my arms to find my sleeves with no holes or gashes anywhere. No sign of injuries or blood that would've freaked me out. But that was how things went, I guess, when you had real people going against unreal monsters.

That said, trying to kill skeletons was still a real pain in the ass, and since I couldn't get my attacker to stand still enough so I could hack away at it till its life points were gone, I decided to tackle it to the ground, feeling a bid creeped out over the fact that while I could do that, the knowledge of its unreality continued to smack my awareness. I let out a yelp and threw myself against the damn thing, pulling it down to the ground, and we both thumped against that weird plastic-y grass, rolling a couple of times with me ending up on top, straddling it, and hacking away at its chest. It was really too bad that there was no way for us to tell how many points were being deducted with each blow. I think it would've helped us out a good deal by making us conserve our energy throughout the fight and not stay on Full Blast Mode from start to finish.

By the time the skeleton died by exploding in a rain of shattered bones under my weight—yeah, that was how skeletons died in this game—I'd already used up my energy, and I was sweaty and panting.

Around me the battle continued, with the heroes either blasting the skeletons with fireballs or pummeling them with power punches. I had to stumble back to my feet, my grip on my knife tightening, as I scanned the area for another monster to destroy. I found one that was emerging from behind Ridley, and I ran toward it, tackling it like before, and straddling it while stabbing its life points away.

By the time the dust cleared, we all stood pretty scattered, surrounded by piles of shattered bones. It didn't hit me till then that I'd just destroyed four skeletons, though I knew the heroes mowed down twice as many each.

"Okay, now what?" Ridley asked, breaking our tired silence.

"Weapons exchange!" I said, hurrying over to a pile of bones when I spotted something lying on the grass next to it. It was a sword this time. I dropped my knife and claimed that without even bothering to think about it. I mean, duh. It was about three feet long, with the blade much, much broader, and it was fairly heavy but still easy to swing around.

I couldn't help but think that the more points I earned, the more masculine I was becoming, judging from the increasing lengths of the swords I was bound to pick up along the way. What a totally Freudian game this was.

I joined everyone else, picking our way through the carnage and looking for clues or whatever else that we needed for this "mission." Freddie found a couple of bottles filled with healing potions, which we agreed we didn't need since the monsters attacking didn't do us any physical damage beyond exhaustion. Peter found a bottle of magic potion—or at least we decided it was something like that, given the amount of sparkles in the liquid—and it was an elixir of some kind that would've empowered a mage when drunk right out of the bottle. I found a leather jerkin, but I didn't need it, obviously.

"Hey, guys, check this out," Wade said, appearing from a cluster of trees, half of which she'd mildly destroyed using her fire balls. Thin black smoke rose up from partially charred branches and leaves. She held a scroll that she'd just unrolled.

Peter took it from her and read it out loud. "'I can communicate this way. Keep fighting to uncover more messages. Sentries are now working with me to get you out.'"

We exchanged excited glances. "Althea!" I said. "This is great! At least she can guide us like this, right?"

Peter nodded, scanning the message. "This is cool," he said, grinning. "I guess when you mess around with a simple game, there's only so much you can do. Althea's way, way too advanced as a walking computer to be kept out so easily."

"Found another!" Ridley crowed, pointing at something lying under the carcass of a werewolf that joined in the fun earlier. He ran over to the rolled piece of paper and snatched it up. He read it on his way back to us. "It says, 'This is like the nerd's ultimate version of Twitter. Can't talk too long when I access. Totally sucks ass.' There's also a post script," he said. "Looks like we're in Sleeping Beauty's cursed kingdom."

"Yep, that'll help." Wade looked around, grinning and rubbing her gloved hands together. "Okay, I'm ready to move forward. I can't wait till we reach the castle and destroy Sleeping Beauty. I've always hated that fairy tale and that useless doormat of a princess."

Girl fight! Yes!

The massive battle earned enough points for the heroes to add to their built-in arsenal. Both Ridley and Peter went a step above just super strength. Ridley got some of his defense power blasts back, and Peter's hyper speed ability was there, but it wasn't at its normal levels yet. Wade got her fire whip, but it was also not as potent as it usually was. Freddie could mask himself more quickly, and while he could access a few more masks he had in his archive thingie, they weren't the ultimate kickass ones that he used for big battles.

And I had a very large sword in my hand. I never felt so manly in my life.

We suspected that, because the ambush we just had was pretty massive and harder to fight off than before, we were getting close to a "safe place" for players. After walking for another ten minutes, we emerged from the forest and found ourselves in a gypsy camp of some kind.

There were colorful caravans parked all over a massive open area beyond the trees. Horses had their own little corral type of thing outside the camp, and a dozen or so gypsies moved around. It was so cool. We all stopped and scoped out the place.

"I guess this is where players would normally tank up on stuff," Freddie said. He'd switched back to his normal self after fighting off skeletons as a ninja with no weapons. Seriously, whatever the hell was Freddie thinking when he decided to create a ninja mask with no über cool weapons? Fail! "You know, buy and sell weapons and gear, stock up on supplies, get a new mission, have sex with one of the locals..."

"Dude, I'm not too sure it's a good idea to share your kinks," Wade said, staring at Freddie, who only gave her a shit-eating grin. She grimaced at that and then flapped her hands at him like she was warding off flies. "Oh, my God, stop planting that idea in my head!"

I looked around me, scrunching my face. "What, no hot gypsies anywhere? What a sad program this is."

So true. Everyone looked like each other up close, the only difference being their costumes. The only things that made some characters stand out were beards for guys and babies being carried around for girls. I wondered if the zombie baby that tried to eat my kneecap used to be a normal baby from this camp. Maybe some witch stole a few and turned them into gross-looking but totally ineffective little monsters to kinda-sorta terrorize the countryside. Yeah, right. Terrorize, my pasty, bony butt.

Peter being Peter, he'd already marched up to someone who looked old and wise and was most likely the camp's leader or something and was talking to him. Or was attempting to, anyway. Peter talked, and the old man just looked at him and then went back to what he was doing, which was stand in front of a tent and smoke a pipe. I didn't know till then that gypsy leaders toked out like that. I should ask Dad and Mom about my granddads and what they *really* used to put inside their pipes back in the day.

"Looks like the game characters can't talk to us," Ridley said as we both stood nearby, watching Peter. Freddie and Wade had wandered off to check out the rest of the camp and look around for more scrolls. "I wonder if that hacker creep did that on purpose."

"Or maybe this is one of the limitations of Althea's hacking," I replied. "She wasn't able to stay in the game long enough to mess with it even more. I can only imagine how things would be if she did." It would've been so cool, I was sure.

Peter sighed, glanced back at us, and shrugged. He then disappeared inside the tent, most likely to see what was there, which only made me wish that we had our own private tent to escape into. But life's never fair, and mine sucked.

"How do we find our way to the castle, then?" I asked, moving on and taking a lazy stroll around the camp with Ridley next to me.

"I'm guessing that the road would be pretty obvious. This game's a basic one to begin with, so I wouldn't be surprised if everything's going to be straightforward and easy—or obvious," he said.

It made sense. That'd be a score in favor of lazy thinking by the game's programmers.

We eventually joined Freddie and Wade, who were both standing just outside the gypsy camp, talking and pointing at different spots in the horizon. Right before them was a big dirt road, which could only mean the way to Sleeping Beauty's cursed castle. Or haunted. Or possessed. What the hell ever. Come to think of it, it wouldn't be accurate calling the princess "Beauty", considering what had likely happened to her. Man, I couldn't wait to see what she *really* looked like.

"We're moving forward," Peter said, panting, as he jogged up to us from behind. "I tried to see if I could communicate with any of the others characters, but no deal. Looks like we're on our own."

"We checked for scrolls and other things that Althea can use to contact us with, but there's nothing here. I guess we'll have to get those along the way, post-carnage," Wade replied.

I looked at everyone. "Are you guys getting bored yet? I am."

They all exchanged glances and either nodded or shrugged. "The fact that we can't get hurt is a good thing," Wade said. "But the game's so linear and simple that there's not a lot of excitement even during the fights." She paused and then backed off, raising both hands up. "Not that I'm saying we're better off getting all hacked up and maimed, of course! I just have a feeling that this is going to be a long adventure for us—if you were to call it that."

"I'm with you," Peter said, looking sheepish. I amazed myself sometimes at how well I was able to read heroes' faces so well even with their masks on. I mean, you know—totally amazed. "We'll have to hack and slash our way to the castle and through it till we get to Sleeping Beauty herself."

We started walking forward. "I wouldn't even call her Beauty anymore," I said when Peter took my hand, and we again fell behind the others. "I mean, can you picture what she looks like right now, being cursed by a demon or something? She probably looks like the love child of a vampire mummy and demon poop—the diarrhea kind."

"Oh, come on, man!" Freddie snapped from the front without looking back. "I really didn't need that!"

I rolled my eyes. "That's like normal conversation at my dinner table every day," I said. "By the way, you guys should come around and meet my family and have lunch or something. My parents would be so thrilled that I actually have a social circle beyond Peter and Althea."

My friends answered me with a scattered, "No thanks." Man, for superheroes, they sure were wimps about diarrhea talk at the dining table.

1. * * *

We went over a stone bridge, which led us to a new area that was completely covered in snow. It was kind of hard still trying to wrap my mind around the fact that we were inside a game, not just playing it, and I had to stop and look behind me to observe what the previous land or kingdom looked like since the snowy landscape we were in now took me by surprise. Yeah, it was all summer-like beyond the bridge.

I wondered if the game programmers were inspired by global warming.

"I don't know about you guys, but I'm so tempted to make a snow angel," Freddie said. He'd stopped and was now looking off to the side, staring at the snow, which rose up to Freddie's height in some places. Sure enough, it wasn't cold at all. "I've never been to a place with snow before."

"We can't mess around, Freddie," Wade said. "We're in a hurry here. Okay, we're bored and in a hurry, but still—there's no time for playing around."

"Two seconds? It'll only take me two seconds."

"It takes you way longer than that to make a snow angel."

"Oh, come on, Wade..."

Wade just sighed, shaking her head. "Look, if we let you mess around like this, chances are, someone else will want to do it, and then another, and then another—"

"And it's all chaos and death," I said.

Freddie frowned at us. He actually frowned. Then he nodded at something that was behind me. "Then how come *he* gets to mess around in the snow?"

I whipped around, suddenly realizing that Peter wasn't standing beside me. Sure enough, about ten feet away was Peter, putting the final touches on a snowman he'd just made. And judging from how complete and impressive it looked even without the eyes, mouth, scarf, and whatever, it was pretty safe to say that he used his hyper speed (whatever levels he'd managed to regain, anyway) to get things done. He was also grinning the whole time he carefully dusted off excess snow and stuff. Okeedokee.

He stepped back, resting his hands on his hips, and surveyed his masterpiece. Then realizing that he was being watched, he quickly turned, his hands dropping to his sides, the loopy grin on his face fading.

"Oh. Hi," he said. "Sorry. I couldn't help myself. Been a while since I played in snow."

He trotted over to us, all flushed and embarrassed but apparently tension-free. Note to self: go through with my plan to buy a custom cottage somewhere in the wilderness, where it snowed, so my husband-to-be could enjoy making snowmen and give me all kinds of awesome fantasies about him and winter.

"I hope that helped get some toxins out of your system," I said when he joined me, and he shrugged, the loopy grin returning. What a dork.

"Well, Peter's got hyper speed powers, so if he wanted to mess around, it'd be okay because he wouldn't be taking up too much time, and—" Wade's words faltered when Freddie let out a loud whoop and threw himself on the ground, rolling around till he was lying face up. Throwing his hands and feet out, he started making a snow angel.

"It's chaos, Wade," I said dully. She stared at Freddie and then me. Then she shook her head.

"Screw it," she said, running off the path to an area that was deep in snow—well, knee-deep, anyway. Bending down, she started gathering snow and shaping it into a ball. She turned, spied Ridley who stood across the way from her, and instantly started a snowball fight with him.

"It's total chaos," I said, pursing my lips as I watched a bunch of superheroes play in the snow and in full costume, too. Including Freddie, who'd transformed himself into a generic vampire count—all dressed in black with the long cape, his fangs poking out as he grinned, still flailing against the snow and completely destroying his snow angel. I think at that point he was so caught up with the energy of the moment that he didn't give a rat's ass about what mask he'd just put on and was playing.

When I realized that Peter had vanished from my side, I sighed and turned around to find him finishing up another snowman, which stood beside the first one he made. Again, thanks to his hyper speed power, he was able to make one in a matter of a few seconds.

The area was filled with happy yells and catcalls from my friends as they continued to mess around for a few more moments. I alternately frowned and then grinned, scratching my head, as I watched them. I guess this was badly needed. They'd been working non-stop since they all came into their powers, and this moment of craziness was something that was bound to happen when you gave them the day off. Eventually I loosened up and watched them like a mom—okay, dad—laughing whenever someone did something stupid or silly. Which was, actually, all of them all of the time.

Before long all four superheroes were engaged in a nutty snowball fight, though no one took sides. Strange, but I somehow felt as though this was their moment and theirs alone. I could've joined in the fun, but my gut told me that this momentary craziness was kind of sacred to them, so I held off and quietly explored the area. They didn't notice me, which was perfectly fine. I didn't want to take them away from their de-stressing moment. I tried to pick my way around them, inching along the periphery and poking my sword between branches of thick shrubs, looking for scrolls or clues or anything to distract myself with.

I didn't see anything weird at first. There was a mountain off to the left of our path, and I followed its base, humming to myself while poking around like the trapped-but-bored gamer that I was. The snow didn't feel cold—like everything else since we started, it was room temperature even though it felt and handled like snow. Every plant and rock was covered with the stuff, and even the mountain's ridges and crevices were dusted with white.

I was just about to go back and rejoin the others when I peered through a large and thick bush that grew at the base of the mountain.

"Oh, check this out!" I said, setting aside my sword and reaching in, hoping that there weren't any dumb zombie babies or small creatures of the night hiding in the shadows.

With a sigh of relief I grabbed hold of the small chest that I'd spotted sitting behind the branches and pulled it out. It looked like a pirate's treasure chest, the way it was designed, but it was about the same width as one of those larger laptops. It was made of wood with discolored metal designs and whachamacallits. It didn't feel heavy, either, which made me suspect that it kept something important. Of course, it could also be totally empty.

"Hey, guys, look at this!"

I carried the chest under one arm and picked up my sword. The others had stopped their game time and were now seated just off the main path, resting. The snow around them—more like within a fifty-mile circle around us (Radical? Radius? Rad, like, totally? Rodent?)—was completely destroyed. There were bald patches, irregular piles of snow, and all kinds of crazy patterns here and there that meant a lot of rolling around had happened. Peter's two snowmen had been practically obliterated, with nothing left but half of what used to be their bases. The heroes themselves were a mess, all dusted with white as though they'd all developed a pretty severe and incurable form of dandruff.

"What's that?" Ridley asked as I sat next to Peter, setting the chest on the ground. "Pirate treasure?" He looked around, a little confused. "Boy, the game's programmers went all over the place in putting this thing together. Pirates in the snow? Yeah, I can see that."

The treasure chest wasn't locked, and I opened it to find a scroll inside. I took it out and showed everyone. "Ta da! Here's another message from Althea!"

I unrolled it and read it out loud without skimming over it first. "'Surprise, losers! Guess who! So I'm sure that by this time, you think this game's way too simple and boring, right? Okay, I'm up for a challenge. It's called hide and seek. By the time you finish reading this message, all but one of you will be left to carry on the so-called mission, which is to reach the castle and destroy all of the monsters there. And here's the twist: for you to win and get out of the game, you'll have to find the other heroes, who'll be turned into things that blend in with the scenery, courtesy of some pretty kickass hacking skills by moi. And you'll have to get all that done in two hours, tops, or you'll be stuck in this game forever, along with your transformed hero friends. So much for boring games, eh? Better start now. The clock's ticking.'"

I glanced up, shocked, and saw that everyone save for Ridley was missing. He sat directly across from me, pale and horrified.

"Oh, my God," he squawked, his head whipping around as he frantically searched the area. "Oh, my God, Eric—where'd they all go?"

"What the hell happened?" I asked, scrambling to my feet and glancing around as well. The place was deserted. The only signs of life that I saw were marks in the snow where Wade, Freddie, and Peter had seated themselves not too long ago.

"I don't know!" he cried, following my lead. "They were sitting with us one minute and then gone the next!"

"Like a transporter got them or something?"

"I think so—but I didn't hear anything. It all happened in a second—literally. Right when you read the last word in that scroll."

"Fuck!" I looked at the message again. "This was another trap, just like that first scroll you found. But if this talked about having only one hero left, why are there two of us here?"

Ridley looked at me, all freaked out. "Dunno—maybe because you're not a superhero? That's all I can think of. I mean, maybe this game's rigged so that only genetically-tweaked people are affected by whatever's been done to it. I'm guessing that you're able to fly under the radar because you're normal."

Panic levels were at a record high as I reread the message a gazillion times over. "Okay, we need to calm down and think," I said, giving him the scroll to go over as well. Chewing my cuticles, I started to pace around Ridley. "I think everyone's been taken to the castle and maybe turned into things, and if we want to get out of here, we need to find them, finish the game, and then be free."

"We can't find them if they're blending in with the scenery! I mean, are there going to be clues anywhere?"

"I know we can't without clues or whatever, but that's what this asshole's saying! He knows it's practically impossible to find them, anyway, and he's banking on that to keep us trapped here!"

"What're we gonna do?"

I stopped my pacing and looked at Ridley, echoing his deer-and-headlights look. "I think we should move forward and keep playing. You need to up your points, anyway, and earn back your powers."

"Yeah, but they're all defense powers. Lot of good that'll be!" Ridley's complexion went white and red and then a funny shade in between that I didn't really want to figure out. Probably puke green with a touch of fuchsia.

"Hey, cut it out," I retorted. "You're way better than that. You've punched your way to higher points, haven't you?" When he nodded helplessly, I added, "There you go. You've got your power punches for offense, and you can shield us or slow monsters down when the going gets way too rough for only two people to deal with."

"I guess so, but I don't know how well that'll all work out."

"The only thing we can do is cross our fingers, kick major ass, and hope for the best." I winced as we exchanged nervous looks again. "One thing we definitely need to do is to supply you with weapons like mine. I mean, a power punch is good, but it's also better to have some offensive backup, right?"

Ridley could only nod, his grip on the scroll tightening as though he were clenching his hand into a frightened fist.

"And we've got Althea hacking into the program once in a while to help us out, though I wish I knew how to talk to her. Communication here's all one-way." Crap. Crap, crap, crap, *crap*.

God, of all people to be left behind—the baby of the superhero bunch, who still needed to work on his game, and the non-superhero with limited-to-zero strength. Oh, man, we were so screwed.

Chapter 8

Ridley and I marched onward, nervous and completely unsure of how we were going to pull this off. I didn't want to add to his issues, but I sure didn't have much faith in his abilities at the moment, given the fact that he was a defense hero. What good were force fields when we needed to fight our way to the castle and destroy everything we saw there? And Ridley had zero confidence to boot, with whatever self-esteem he had taking a pretty massive beating when we were first trapped in this game.

I sighed, staring ahead and keeping an eye out for stray monsters here and there that I could slaughter, so we could up our points as quickly as we could. I tried not to think about Peter and the fact that he'd just been turned into something that we could easily overlook and leave behind because he'd become a part of the scenery. That thought was enough to make me want to curl up on the ground and fall asleep, hoping to wake up and find myself safe in my bedroom with Grimm, lost in happy denial.

But at the same time, I knew that that denial thing would be something that Peter hated, and I could hear his voice lecturing me in my head. If I were more emotional, I'd have fallen apart and got all wobbly-lipped and sniffly, but I was pissed. I mean, *pissed*. Like Mrs. Zhang-style pissed when she was turned into a toddler by the Deathtrap Debutantes. The more I wallowed in the fact that my boyfriend and my other buddies had been turned into game accessories, the angrier I got. I wanted to kick monster ass so badly, bust out of the freakin' game, and majorly kick that jerk hacker's ass till his sphincter fused itself with his brain.

I cussed under my breath and shook those thoughts off. I needed to focus and work fast. The first objective I had was to find Ridley a weapon he could use to complement mine as well as his regular defense powers.

The path we took led us up the side of the mountain, where a little gang of wolves came after us. They leaped out from a higher part of the path, oddly not sliding off the edge of the mountain considering how narrow the path was. Then again, that was all part of the game, right? It was pretty damned weird, looking at a pack of wolves snarling and snapping away at us, with a couple of them standing off the side of the mountain path and looking as though they were on an invisible ledge.

"Okay, whatever," I said, holding up my sword and taking my position. "You ready, Ridley?"

"Yeah," he said. Too bad he stammered, which kind of threw me off my anger mojo for a moment. But he also assumed the position, raising both his fists in front of him like an old-school boxer.

"Just punch the hell out of them."

"Easy for you to say. It's so weird, punching a fake wolf to death like this."

"I know. The things we put up with when trapped inside a game."

The wolves lunged at us, snapping their jaws and making as though they were ripping us to shreds. As with the previous monsters, we didn't feel anything but soft rubber moving whenever they came into contact with us, but it didn't change the fact that two against six was kinda-sorta unfair. Besides, with us advancing with every kill, the wolves were also harder to get rid of compared to the previous monsters.

I barely kept track of Ridley, who quickly got into his battle zone, and as I swung my sword again and again till I could feel my shoulders crack, I heard him let out angry grunts and occasional cries of "Take that! And that! Ha!"

Well, if he got into our battles in that same mindset he was in when he was doing all those practice search-and-rescue missions with the others, yelling out virtuous catch phrases along the way, that was perfectly cool with me. Every once in a while, I'd hear a wolf howl, which was the sign of death.

For my part, I hacked away, having been backed up against the mountain wall by two wolves. Gritting my teeth and letting out angry, virtuous sounds as I fought, I swung my weapon like crazy, listening to my sword whistle in the air and watching obviously fake blood fly all over the place till one wolf howled before collapsing. Then I continued with the second wolf, which didn't take too long for me to kill. After it howled, it fell off to the side, and I was standing in between two fake-bloodied carcasses. Half of their bodies floated outside the path, by the way, and I shook my head at how bizarre it all looked.

It was quiet now, with nothing but heavy pants and gasps filling the air. I glanced up and found Ridley at the top of the path, which was a level surface. He was all red and sweaty, but he looked elated at the same time. I saw that he'd slaughtered four wolves to my two.

"Tsk," I muttered, making a face as I trudged up the path to join him. "The downside to being genetically normal."

When I reached him, I gave him a high five. "Good job! Too bad I suck at fighting. It's like I can't kill more than maybe a quarter of what you kill, and even then, I'm wasted." I shook my head, grinning tiredly, while wiping my forehead against my sleeve.

"I've been thinking about that, actually, and I find that kinda weird," he said after pausing for a moment, scrunching up his face in concentration. "I suppose we can blame superhero powers for that, but my fighting skills feel—well, they feel pretty basic. You know, generic. So in a way, we should be fairly even as far as damage points go."

I snorted, still grinning. "Yeah, sure, generic for you, maybe, but not me. You'd still have way stronger fighting skills than I ever can, no matter what, because of who you are."

Ridley didn't look convinced. "I don't know, Eric. Gut feeling tells me that there's something else that's up, and what we get out of these mini-battles says as much."

I shrugged. "At this point, it doesn't matter to me. If my killing a quarter of what you're able to kill somehow helps you, I'm cool with that. At least I don't stand by, all helpless and stuff. Come on, let's look for more messages from Althea."

So we busied ourselves for the next few moments looking around for scrolls. After finding another bottle of healing potion and another leather vest, we decided to move forward and continue battling it out.

I couldn't help but mull over what Ridley just said, though. I didn't feel anything weird, frankly, but I'd always expected fights between me and any monster to be much harder than those between the heroes and monsters. It was pretty much a given in real life, anyway, so why would it be any different in a make-believe world like this?

We walked on, following the path that continued to go up the mountainside. Here and there, we'd be waylaid by wolves and an occasional abominable snowman-type of monster. Or at least it made me think of the abominable snowman because it was like ten feet tall and shaggy-haired. Like a monster hippie without the awesome bling. The attacks were getting more frequent, I noticed, and I was getting tired. Not enough recovery time in between them, and as before, I could only manage to slaughter a fraction of what Ridley could with his bare fists.

"Okay, time out," I panted after our last mini-battle. I had to plop my sorry ass down on a rock, using my sword like a cane that I could lean on while I rested. "Jeebus, this shit's getting harder and harder for me."

Ridley stood nearby, watching me and looking sympathetic. But he also looked winded, though I was sure it had everything to do with the fact that he'd killed about eight wolves and abominable snowmen-type things, while I only managed three. And one of them was, like, diseased or something, judging from its fur's coloring and its scarred, zombie-like face. I mean, seriously? That was pretty sad.

"I wish I could give you extra strength or recovery time," Ridley said. "I wouldn't even trust those healing potions we find. They look like sparkly blood inside bottles."

I shuddered. "Hell, no, I'm not touching those! I'd rather fight using my own strength than down any of that stuff."

"Okay, let's rest for a bit. I don't know how much longer we have till we reach the castle, but we can't stay here too long. I'm going to look around."

I nodded, and Ridley walked away to explore. In the meantime, I felt all depressed as I started to really consider what my role was. It felt as though I wasn't part of the game—not sure exactly how I came up with that conclusion, but circumstances kind of made me entertain that idea even though there wasn't anything conclusive about them. I just had a way harder time fighting monsters, and that was that, though I probably should blame Ridley for planting the seeds in my head to begin with.

I leaned my head against my sword's hilt, gulping air and listening to my heart slow down its beating. I was also getting really, really hungry, which upset me, because I knew that it meant my energy stores were practically zero. Hell, they were most likely in the negative numbers by now, judging from how I felt.

"I found something!" Ridley called out. I didn't even bother to stand up when he came back into view, waving not one, but three rolled up pieces of paper.

"Meh. Could be another trap."

"Could be a message from Althea."

"I'll betcha it's a trap."

Ridley snorted as he unrolled one scroll while dumping the other two on the ground. "You're too cynical."

"Considering what's been happening, can you blame me? This sucks!" I leaned against my sword again, but I kept my eyes on him. I might be cynical, but I was still open to possible good news.

Ridley quietly read the message first, and he broke out into a smile. "Told you it's good news," he said, glancing up at me. "Message from Althea: 'Tracking your progress. Found some weird scars in the program. Communicating those to Sentries.'"

I nodded, my mood lifting. "What about the others?"

Ridley stooped down to pick up the other two scrolls and unrolled the second one. "Dude, check this out: 'Game doesn't seem to acknowledge Eric. He doesn't register anywhere in the program. I think hacker only expected heroes, or he didn't know how to tweak game to mark non-hero.'"

We looked at each other, frowning. "Well, I guess that's good news, depending on what that means," I stammered, scratching my head. "If the game doesn't recognize me, that explains why I feel like I'm like salmon going upstream when I fight. But then what?"

Ridley shrugged, looking just as confused as me. "Let's see what the third scroll says: 'Communicating like Twitter sucks ass, but keep moving.'"

"That's it? A mini-bitchfest about communicating in limited characters?" I retorted, and Ridley shrugged again. I sighed as I watched him roll up the scrolls again and then stare at them. "Okay, fine. Looks like Althea confirmed what you said about something else going on—at least where I'm concerned. But what about that? If the game doesn't recognize me even if I fight against monsters and stuff, how's that going to help us?"

"I don't know. I have a feeling it means that you don't earn us points when you kill something."

"What th—you mean all that trouble for nothing? How fucked up is that?"

"That's how the game responds to you, dude. If monsters react to you, it's because you get in their way, not because you're that hacker's target. It's pretty normal for monsters in computer games to do that."

I frowned even more. "So you mean I should stay away from what's attacking us?" Okay, at that point my brain hurt so much, I needed to hunt down that zombie baby if only to kick it again and again. Maybe even see if I could dribble it around like a disgusting basketball.

Ridley grimaced when he paused. "Oh, man, this sucks. This means that only I can earn points, no matter what you do to help me fight my way to the castle."

I shook my head, getting even more pissed than ever. "Oh, hell, no. That's not gonna fly. If the program doesn't recognize me, it should work for us somehow. We just have to figure stuff out along the way."

"But here's our problem now—if you can't earn us points, it means you'll have to stop fighting in order to give me all of the monsters I can kill to earn maximum points, right? But that's going to slow us down along the way with only a couple of hours to get through the castle. I mean, you're helping me out a lot by taking care of some monsters..."

I stood up, sighing heavily, and took up my sword. "No, I'm not going to buy that, Ridley. We have to figure out what I can do as a—dunno—non-entity in this game. I'm sure that this is going to help us somehow." I walked up to him and gave him a tired but encouraging pat on the shoulder. "That jerk might think that he's managed to get you, but it looks like he didn't really think certain things through. Or he probably just totally screwed up in his own hacking to have this kind of glitch."

Ridley didn't answer, but he turned and faced a tree that was several feet away. Raising both hands, he let the scrolls drop as he focused, and his hands immediately glowed with pulsing energy. With a little cry that sounded like *"Wah!"* Ridley blasted the tree with an energy bubble, completely swallowing it up.

We both stared at it for a moment, counting seconds before it faded, and I nearly pissed my pants in excitement to see that the bubble remained for a long time before it went away. Ridley had amassed enough points to access his more advanced defense powers, at least.

"Okay, if time's our enemy right now, we definitely need to get you weapons," I said, turning to him. "Power punches are great, but if you want to kill as many as you can in the shortest amount of time, something fast and effective would be good." I thought for a moment before blurting out, "A crossbow! Yeah, that'll be good. Range weapons should work."

Ridley nodded, looking a bit stunned yet elated at having close-to-normal levels of superpowers back. I led him away, once again following the path that meandered through the snow. "I've never used crossbows before. I hope the learning curve isn't too steep."

"Nah. I'm sure you've got natural talent in slaughtering things at a distance."

"That's good to know, I guess."

"Hey, at least you're not doing this for nothing. Look at me, all manly and stuff with this big-ass, overcompensating-for-something sword, and I don't even get us any points." I had to pause. "Oh, God, this game's like my own life, isn't it?"

Ridley just looked at me glumly. "I guess we'd better move forward."

I *so* wanted that zombie baby back.

* * * *

Ridley and I hacked our way through a couple more ambushes, but we tried a different tactic both times. Ridley zapped monsters in pairs, pretty much trapping them in force fields, while he methodically picked through those that he didn't cocoon. Sometimes it was three monsters against one hero. Those he couldn't tackle, I hacked at, and once those were killed, he "popped" one force field with a small power blast, freeing the monsters inside, so we could get at them. Then the process started all over again.

It was annoyingly slow that way, and I was seriously getting all freaked out over the time, but with Ridley being the only "character" in the game that the program was recognizing, he needed to control the attacks as much as he could, and temporarily trapping monsters in those energy bubbles was the only thing we could think of. I guess one good thing about this method was seeing Ridley's confidence as well as the strength of his punches increase. That was probably the only offensive power he had since he was a defense hero, but it was better than nothing.

In the meantime, I kept an eye out for new weapons to take and for crossbows to show up in the carnage.

The last group of monsters we destroyed attacked us right before another bridge, which was guarded by some generic-looking CGI dude in generic-looking peasant clothes.

"He's not going to talk to us," I panted, leaning on my sword after slaughtering a massive, demon-possessed wild boar-like thing that had one eye. Was there such a thing as a mutant wild boar Cyclops? Because that was totally mental.

"He's in the way," Ridley said, also gasping for breath.

"Push the bastard off the cliff, then," I said, shaking my head. "Serves him right for standing in the way and blocking traffic."

Ridley gave me a look. It kind of reminded me of the look that Mom would give me when she mentally threatened me with an adult-strength wedgie. On Ridley, the look pretty lost some steam because he wasn't psychotic like mothers.

"Okay, fine, let me see if I can talk to him," I said, trudging forward and using my sword like a walking stick. And what a kickass walking-stick it made, too. All that was missing was an equally kickass backpack that hikers used—only totally juiced up or something to match the sword. If we were to come across another gypsy camp along the way, I was *so* going to ransack the hell out of that place and steal a cool pack. Who was going to arrest me, anyway? I was a nonentity in the game. So there.

I glanced back over my shoulder to find Ridley busying himself with picking through the monster corpses for scrolls or weapons. He was really getting into the game, I could tell.

I sighed once I reached the generic dude, staying quiet for a moment as I tried to take in details. Yep, he was generic, all right. Tallish, bulky (like all peasants or laborers were bulky, right?), dressed in clothes that you only see in Renaissance Fairs, beard the color of medieval men's beards (what the hell shade was it—baby diarrhea?), small, shifty eyes. Not sure if those small, shifty eyes could actually see me, but they seemed to work okay.

"Uh..." I paused, scrunching my face. How did someone address a CGI character in person, anyway? "Hi. How's it going?" Oh, this was stupid. I felt my face burn even though I was sure no one could see me squirming and blushing and wishing that no one could see me. "Listen, would you mind stepping aside, so my friend and I can go through? We're kind of in a hurry to get to the cursed castle."

The guy stood there for a moment, moving or shifting his weight and repositioning his arms the way these game characters moved while they waited in the background. And the movements were repetitive, which was pretty typical in games.

I sighed, pursing my lips. I kind of figured it wasn't going to work. I was going to turn around and talk to Ridley when the generic dude suddenly talked.

"You need to wait here for reinforcements," he said in a low, robotic monotone—again, like the way these characters sounded when they talked to your avatars. Or at least like in those low-end type of games that I was familiar with because those were all I could afford. You know, poverty-level schoolboy thing and stuff.

"Oh, my God!" I yelped, jumping back and instantly holding up my sword in front of me. "He talked! Ridley! He's possessed!"

"It won't take long. Be patient," he said. He didn't look at me like he saw me or anything. He continued to do those repetitive movements like a good, obedient CGI character.

Ridley had run up to me by then, and we both gaped at the guy. Then we looked at each other, still gaping.

"Whoa," he breathed. "He heard you?"

"I don't know. He might've sensed me, though, because he started talking after I talked first. But I thought that the game can't recognize me? I don't get it."

"You need help. You can't do this alone. Two characters are on the way," the guy said, still moving and fidgeting and stuff. Add that to the low, lifeless voice and the fact that the character could communicate with us—I was surprised that I didn't have a coronary right then and there.

"Um—Althea?" Ridley stammered, leaning a little closer. I kept my sword in front of me, ready for slaughter.

"I can possess characters now, but not all," Mr. Generic Peasant said. It was Althea trying to reach us! "I can't hear you still, but I can sense your presence."

"Damn. And I was hoping that we'd be able to have a back-and-forth conversation with her," I muttered, sighing and lowering my sword. My breath caught in my throat. "Wait—what reinforcements? A couple of characters? What?"

Ridley shook his head, but I saw that while he was just as confused as I was, he also seemed to be excited. "Don't know, but I'm crossing my fingers. All we can do right now is trust her."

"Okay, but I'm seriously worried about the time. I don't know how much we have left. I hope we don't have to wait too long, or we're all screwed."

"I wouldn't worry," Ridley said, slapping my shoulder and sounding way more chipper than he did before. "Althea said that the Sentries are now involved. Knowing that helps."

"They're almost here," Mr. Generic Peasant said.

"Man, I hope this isn't another trap," I grumbled, turning around and gripping my sword firmly without raising it up in defense. "I'm really regretting messing around with the idea of giving Peter a souped-up video game for his birthday. Hell, I'm plain regretting that I've even heard of video games. After today, I'm giving up these damn things forever."

"Let's hope it's not another trap."

"They're here!" Mr. Generic Peasant said, sounding oddly excited despite his low, robotic monotone.

The area where we had our last fight was unsurprisingly free of monster corpses now. Nothing but a clear path flanked by snowdrifts, rocks, leafless trees, and bald shrubs stretched out behind us. For a moment, nothing happened. I was going to turn to Ridley and bitch about psychological manipulation in video games when a couple of figures appeared from the shadows of trees, walking quickly up the path toward us.

I stared at them in shock. They were a couple of CGI characters, all right, both of whom were dressed differently from any of the characters we'd seen so far, which made me think that they were characters that were being actively played by someone out there. Both were female, with one dressed in green and dark gray, all slender and tall with black hair pulled back in a ponytail. She also wore a cloak with its hood hanging down in dark green, and she was armed with a massive bow. As for her arrows, I'd no idea where she kept them, but this being a video game, I was sure that she had magical never-ending supplies of arrows that would appear somehow.

The other was just as tall but was also bulkier, and she was dressed more like a knight—all in silver armor with a gray cape. She was a redhead, her hair curling out from under a silver helm. She held a pretty impressive-looking sword and a shield.

Ridley and I exchanged confused looks, but we held our ground and waited for them to come closer. They didn't give off any danger vibes, seeing as how they were obviously designed to be heroes.

The two women stopped in front of us and took on the same monotonous movements as the Generic Medieval Peasant. They just stood there, swaying while turning their heads left and right, their hands still gripping their weapons.

"Hi, Eric," the archer said, her voice a low monotone as well. It was clear that the voice was from the game itself and was probably how the characters sounded like to each other. So freakin' bizarre. "It's Trini. I've been recruited to help."

"I'm Dario," the knight said, her voice the same as the archer's. "Nice to meet you, finally. Well, kind of. This isn't exactly how I look, though I wish."

I gaped at both, the only part of my body moving at that moment being my eyeballs as I stared at the archer first and then the knight.

"Whoa," I said after swallowing. "What the hell?"

"I had to recruit them," the Generic Peasant guy behind us piped up, nearly making me piss my pants. I'd completely forgotten that he was there. I wished I had a prescription for heart pills because this was getting way too much for mine. "I had to out myself to them. Trini, can you see two people there?"

"Yeah, I can," the archer replied. "Dario?"

"I can see them both, too."

"They can communicate with each other!" I said and then paused. "Oh, of course, they can. If Trini and Dario are now involved, it means that they're in the same room as Althea."

"And our identities as heroes aren't a secret anymore," Ridley said.

"Oh, no. This can only mean one thing," I whispered, turning to him, in case Trini and Dario's avatars could hear us. "Once we're done with the game, the Sentries will be zapping them both to clear their memories and save your identities."

He looked just as anxious as I felt. "I'm sure they know what they're doing. They might be a covert group, but they're not here to hurt anyone. Trini and Dario should be fine if they do get their memories tampered with."

"Yeah, but how much of an effect would that have? I've heard of repressed memory incidents. This might come back to haunt them, like, years from now."

Ridley sighed. "Eric, there's nothing we can do. Someone made the decision to help us, and we have to play along even if we don't agree with it. Let's just get the hell out of here and then worry about what comes after."

I grimaced. "Man, you're sounding like a mini-Magnifiman. That's creepy."

"Testing, testing," Trini's archer spoke, but when she kept repeating those words another dozen or so times, I heard a change in her tone. "Guys, I'm getting Althea to change my voice, so Dario and I won't sound alike, and you don't have to look at either of us to know who's talking. Testing, testing. A couple more notes higher, I think? Testing. Yeah, that's it. That's good."

Sure enough, the archer's voice kept getting lighter and lighter till she sounded a little like a young girl, not a badass adult female warrior. But I could see Trini's point. With the game coming with pre-recorded voices that were probably only two kinds—male and female—it'd be way helpful for us to know who was talking in the middle of a fight or just plain traveling.

"Okay, is everyone ready?" Mr. Generic Peasant asked. "Trini and Dario are now locked in with Ridley, so you'll all be earning points as a group. Eric, keep fighting as backup to help. I'm sure there are tons of things for you to do as a kinda-sorta ninja-esque character in the game."

"I kind of like that, now that I think about it," I said, my mood lifting.

"Let Dario lead you since he's the knight and has the highest damage points. Trini and Ridley can work together for range offense and defense. You guys aren't far from the castle now. It's past the bridge."

I stared at the bridge and the meadow that stretched out beyond that. "Wow, so soon? How many kingdoms did we slaughter our way through? Three at most? This is a pretty short game if that's the case." Man, what a rip-off this game turned out to be.

"In case you're wondering, I was able to shorten the game time by deleting another ten or so kingdoms you needed to pass through. I don't know how the next kingdom will look after what I did, but be ready for some crazy-ass action," Mr. Generic Peasant said. "Our hacker didn't really think about that. Score for me, bitches!"

"If that's the case, then we're all below the skill level needed to hack our way through to the castle," Trini piped up. "This is going to be tough."

"Then again, the higher the life points of the monsters we kill, the faster it'll be for us to level up," Dario replied. "Yeah, it'll be tough to fight our way through, but if we're all coordinated, we should survive all the way to the castle."

That totally didn't sound good to me. Ridley would be a great help whenever he used his force fields, but still—I was the weakest one in the group that was made up of "characters" who were in over their heads. What the hell was going to happen to me? It was cold comfort that I couldn't be killed, and I wouldn't be surprised if I could only manage to kill one monster per ambush, considering the massive difference in life points we'd have between us.

"Man," I grumbled. "Maybe I can run around like crazy, tire out all those advanced monsters, and let them lose their life points from exhaustion. Oh—no, wait. They're CGI monsters. They don't get tired. I will."

"Eric, I might not see you, but I can sense you kicking up the drama meter," Mr. Generic Peasant said, and I rolled my eyes and flipped him off. "I sensed that, too, ass munch."

Chapter 9

We all managed to squeeze around that stupid generic dude, whom Althea somehow couldn't manipulate to get out of our damn way. What was up with that? She could delete a gazillion kingdoms and merge the last one with the place where we happened to be, but she couldn't make a stupid generic peasant move out of our way? Whatever. But we trooped along, with Dario's knight taking the lead as planned, Ridley behind her, Trini behind Ridley, and me taking up the rear because, you know, I was like the pathetic little non-entity in the group.

If my sword could accurately reflect my standing, it'd be drooping in my hands, not straightened out in a big, hard line. You know, come to think of it, that'd also be a pretty accurate picture of my sexual relationship with Peter: a wilted sword. All that was missing was stuff like moss or black mold.

Maybe I should get back into writing haikus again because that was, like, an inspired mental image. Depressing, but inspired.

When we set foot in the new kingdom, the changes nearly steamrolled us over. It was like, BAM! This weird, invisible force swept over us like some kind of freak warm wind that felt more solid than airy. I mean, yeah, the land looked normal for a game, but the vibes were way, way off. I could feel that we were definitely in over our heads this time, and because of the deleted stages—or whatever the hell gamers called all those places they had to go through to level up—everything felt majorly cockeyed.

I didn't think that Trini and Dario felt anything. I mean, duh—they were only avatars. But Ridley and I sure did. We stood there for a moment, blinking, shaking our heads as though we were trying to unsee some pretty gross and totally inappropriate thing that we just saw.

"Does it feel like we're walking on a surface that's sort of angled?" I asked, frowning at him. "Because that sure as hell what it feels like."

"Kind of, yeah. Took me a moment to get used to it. You ready?"

I let out a breath and held up my sword, for what it was worth. "Yeah, I guess so. You'll have to excuse me if I only manage to hack off some demon-possessed troll's arm at best. At least I'll make it easier for you to kill him off."

Ridley grinned but didn't say anything, and when he turned to jog off, following Dario's knight, I actually felt better. I still kept my grip on my sword tight, feeling myself tensing up like a coil that was slowly being squished right before letting it go for some pretty devastating spring action.

Okay, so that was a weak way of describing it, but that was still a hundred times better than comparing myself to a Slinky.

The meadow we walked through looked cool, which I figured was nothing more than a danger sign regarding the levels of carnage that we were now going to experience. I still had no idea how much time we had left, but in a way, it was good to stay ignorant because it only fed my determination to get to the dumb castle as soon as possible and save my boyfriend's ass, so I could be all over it once we got the hell out.

Since I was in the back of the four-pack, I watched Trini's archer in front of me, wondering just how good she and Dario were as gamers if they were able to advance so quickly and catch up with us. I suppose it was safe to say that they freakin' kicked *ass*. Then again, I had zero concept of time while stuck in the game, and what might pass for five minutes here could easily have been thirty minutes out there.

"Heads up!" Dario called back after the road turned past a small forest-like collection of trees.

"Oh, my God, here we go," I muttered, swallowing, as we all stopped and got ready. "I'm so screwed."

Ahead of me, the knight held up her sword, Ridley's fists glowed with a soft light, and the archer fitted an arrow—that appeared from nowhere, I swear to God. A series of roars suddenly broke the silence, and sure enough, from the trees a horde of zombie peasants came shambling out. Unfortunately none of them were of the torso-and-above-only species that I liked, which meant that there was no way in hell I was going to be able to outrun any of them.

Incidentally, when I say "shambled," it was more like "staggered forward at ten miles per hour, flailing, drooling, and roaring." I mean, seriously—I thought zombies didn't have much coordination or had issues with their motor skills because they were, you know, totally dead and barely functional. These zombies were like high as a kite while on fast forward.

"Ridley!" I yelled, and Ridley quickly targeted those zombies at the back, zapping them with force fields that kept them from moving forward while letting the first five or so go for the attack.

Then he and the knight charged forward, throwing themselves at the monsters. The archer stood her ground, shooting arrows here and there, and I saw how hard it was going to be, destroying those mofos, given our newbie point levels or whatever the hell you called them. What she did was shoot randomly at advancing zombies, taking out as many life points as she could with each arrow on each monster without killing it. Being handicapped in terms of points, her arrows most likely only took out tiny amounts. But since she never stopped, those arrows continued to chip away at those life points so that, by the time those zombies got to us, I was able to run forward and hack at them. And she was also able to slightly disable those that Ridley and the knight went head-to-head with, making it a little easier for them to destroy them.

"Look for health potions!" Trini's archer said. "Save those—we'll need them!"

I couldn't answer. I was too busy slashing away at one zombie after another, gritting my teeth and swinging my sword again and again, kind of wishing that I took fencing lessons or something that would've made my technique a hell of a lot more efficient. Since I was totally clueless about sword fighting, I just let complete revulsion toward the undead become my energy feeder, so to speak.

"Ugh! You're a lot more disgusting up close than I thought! Die! *Die!*" I cried, gasping and panting, practically blinded by the sweat that poured down my face as I kept my sword moving. I mean, really—what we were fighting against were way grosser than the ones that attacked us at the beginning. Those ones were more like a horde of corpses that looked alike. They were all gray and red, all bald, hissing, groaning, skeletal, with like oozing sores all over their naked bodies. Yeah, even the half-zombies were like that.

These ones were still dressed, and they were a mixture of male and female corpses. So it was like a whole village was turned into the undead or something like that. And up close, they looked more rotten and gross. It was all red and gray, sure, with nothing but white eyeballs for eyes, missing noses because those things must've already fallen away as though they were infected with leprosy, and their mouths were nothing more than ragged gaping holes that were mushy and bloody and dripped slime. Some of them even had their bellies ripped open, so that their innards hung out. I mean—totally disgusting.

Some of those things even dropped body parts behind them. I saw a growing trail of severed arms or hands. I'm not sure, but I thought that a couple of the female zombies left a trail of shriveled, rotting boobs.

It was like living through an actual nightmare, and the only good thing about this was that I couldn't get killed. But I was growing way, way, *way* tired, and it sucked. This was only the first ambush out of—what—three gazillion ones before we got screwed in the castle? Man, I swear I was seriously earning more than my share of that promised pizza.

The CGI world spun around me as I fought, gasping and snarling and spitting out curses, my body twisting and tumbling, rolling on the ground and stumbling back upright. There were so many zombies to kill, and they surrounded us even though Ridley let small numbers free from his force fields. I tried at first to keep slashing away at the nearest zombies I could reach to cut down their life points even more, but it was like the fight never ended.

"Are we there yet?" I cried in between offing—finally!—some freaky-ass armless woman who was sure to give me nightmares for the next year or so and a zombified old man who kind of looked like my former Algebra teacher. I only managed to catch a few breaths before forcing myself to lunge forward and go after that vile-looking undead scumbag. "Anybody here pack some energy drinks? God, this sucks!"

It seriously did. My arms hurt from all that exertion, and my legs were starting to cramp up from running, dodging, leaping, crawling—whatever! And those damned monsters kept showing up—okay, it was Ridley's efforts at popping those force fields of his to release the next group to slaughter.

I managed to down that old zombie guy and stumble away for a moment to catch my breath. I looked around to see how the others were doing.

Dario's knight was majorly kicking undead ass, though she had to stop every once in a while to pull out a flask of health potion and then gulp it all down before picking up where she left off, slashing and stabbing at zombies. Ridley stood several feet away, alternately zapping stray monsters that they couldn't fight off at the moment and using his power punches to kill them. It was awesome watching him punch and zap and dodge any hits that came at him. He looked super confident and, above all, really quick on his feet. I could still remember those jerks in the street taunting him ages ago because of his weight; I wondered what they'd say now with Ridley's cool superhero reflexes on full display.

Trini's archer ran back and forth, sometimes circling us while shooting away. She was way more agile than everyone else, but maybe that had something to do with the fact that she was a range warrior. Maybe archers were naturally light on their feet and able to avoid danger with their lack of armor and muscles.

"Eric! We've got the monsters down to a good number. Look for health potions, quick!" Trini said, and I was only too happy to obey because, man, I was *so* over it by now.

Keeping a tight grip on my sword, I ran around, poking at bodies and searching nearby areas for treasure that popped out whenever a monster was killed. I spotted about five health potions and two magic ones, and I quickly collected the health potions and left them in a group in the middle of the battle.

"Trini! I found some!" I called out. "Oh, shit. Phooey. I forgot—they can't hear me." I made a face as I watched Dario kill a zombie, take a swig out of another health potion he carried, and then run forward to attack another pair of monsters. I glanced down at the health potions. Both Trini and Dario could see them from where they played, anyway. They should be able to collect them whenever they needed to replenish their strength.

The zombie number had been whittled down to about five by now, and it looked like everyone had a good handle on the fight, so I decided to poke around some more. I found a couple of swords that were much shorter than what I had, but they came as a pair, so I assumed that they were über knives that I could use in battle. Since they were shorter and narrower, I guessed that their damage speed was faster than a broadsword's, which would make up for the fact that their damage points were also most likely less.

"I'll take them," I muttered, dropping my sword and picking the knives up. I felt safer like this, anyway, not being weighed down by a weapon that was big and heavy. It'd also help me lower the life points of monsters the way Trini's archer did, as long as I kept stabbing them and preparing them for death blows coming from Dario and Ridley.

As I explored the carnage, I found more health potions and gathered them for my friends.

"Done!" Ridley crowed from somewhere, and I looked around to find him raising both fists—which still glowed—in the air and hopping in place. Sort of like a boxer after a knockout. "We did it!"

The knight and the archer didn't say anything, but they quickly ran to the spot where I dumped all of the health potions I found, and they started hoarding and refueling. I left them to do whatever they needed to do and trotted over to Ridley.

"Good job, man!" I said, giving him a high five. "How was it? Did you feel anything different from the last fights? I mean—other than the fact that there were way more monsters than usual, and they were harder to kill."

Ridley was sweating, I saw. His face was flushed and wet, his hair damp. Oddly, his superhero costume showed nothing at all—no wet spots around the neck, chest, back, armpits, or even crotch areas. Maybe the spandex used for that was from the future or something, and if so, maybe the Sentries would allow me to beg for a wardrobe that wouldn't show just what kind of sweaty, sticky activities I engaged in with Peter. I mean, you know—considering the fact that he and I were still dressed up whenever we fooled around the way desperate virgins fooled around...

"Yeah, they were much harder, and they freakin' wore me out," he said, grinning. "But I could feel myself get stronger much more compared to when we first started out."

I frowned. "You mean it's like earning those life points or something? Like you're leveling up really quickly?"

"Yeah. Isn't that crazy? I can actually feel it! It's like I'm not only getting my powers back, but I'm also adding to them. I wish we could see just how many points we rack up with each punch or something. It'd be cool, knowing how much life points or experience we're gaining each time."

"That sounds awesome. I wish I could feel the same thing," I said, nodding. "But since I'm like a ghost in this game, all I can do is pick up better weapons along the way."

Ridley gave me a playful punch on the shoulder. "That's better than nothing. And you're helping us out, for sure, even if you don't add to our points."

I glanced back and found the archer and the knight at rest—both of them went down on one knee, their heads bowed, and I guessed that it was because they were trying to get some of their energy back.

"Give us another moment, guys," Dario said. "We're trying to save our health potions by not drinking them, and we're bringing our life points back up by resting for a bit."

There you go. Made sense. What a strange combo we all made. If only real life worked that way, too; it'd be so much easier getting a crap load of work done just by stepping aside and resting till I felt my life points go back up to maximum levels. For now, I depended on siesta or coffee, which didn't really amount to much in the long run. Then again, in the real world, I wasn't slashing like crazy at zombies every half hour. Unless you counted older sisters, that is.

I sighed. "I hope I can hold up till the end," I said, giving Ridley a worried little smile. "I can't renew myself the way CGI characters can. I need food. I'm totally starving right now."

"Same here," he said, grimacing and petting his belly. "My stomach was growling the whole time I was fighting. I was glad that no one could hear me."

I glanced down and fixed my gaze on a random zombie corpse—I mean, a dead undead corpse. Yeah, that. It lay a couple of feet away from me, and it was nasty as all hell. At this point, though, I'd gotten so used to looking at disgusting things that I started to zone out, my eyes glazing over even as I stared at the monster.

Then its head turned to look at me, all white eyeballs and bloody, slimy mouth, noseless face, and shit. "Heads up!" it said in a low, gravelly voice.

"Ridley! It's still alive! Kill it! Kill it!" I cried, jumping back and pointing at it with one of my knives. "Pound it till its brains explode!"

"Eric, I can freakin' sense you screaming your head off. Now cut it out!" the zombie retorted. It didn't get up or anything, thank God, but it looked way too similar to Linda Blair's head when it rotated on its axis in *The Exorcist*. Seriously, I was going to kick Althea's ass when I saw her next because this was *so* not cool, and I almost swallowed my tongue. Then again, if I did, that might've taken care of the hunger bit for me, but I was never too keen on self-cannibalism.

Yeah, I'd have to kick her ass.

"Okay, calm down, calm down," Ridley said, looking just as pale as I did. See? I wasn't the only one Althea freaked out. "Let's listen to what she has to say."

"Okay, numb nuts—the castle's another ten minutes away. You've got another ambush coming. I can't get rid of those monsters in case you're wondering. They're sort of like your key to get in the castle to save the others. Just fight them, rest, and move on. The Sentries and I are close to a solution, which isn't a hard one, really, but it's still a pain in the ass to work into this dumb game." The zombie paused, still fixing its eyeballs at me. I desperately wanted to poke them out of their sockets with my knives, but we needed that stupid thing functional, I guess. "The good thing about this is that I can communicate better with you guys now. No more stupid Twitter-like messages, and no more depending on random scrolls."

"Yeah, but it's still a one-way deal," I muttered. "Big whoop."

"I sensed that!"

"Oh, shut up."

At that moment the archer and the knight appeared, with the knight moving past us. "I guess we'd better get moving," Dario said.

I followed them, taking up the rear as usual, but at least I was a little more encouraged by the fact that I now had a couple of kickass weapons that were way faster than the one I had before. I couldn't wait to try them out, for sure, but I was also growing more and more aware of exhaustion and soreness. As we walked down the road, I couldn't help but look around me, my eyes zoning in on a fruit-bearing shrub or something that looked like it, wishing that things worked the way they did in Willy Wonka's chocolate factory, and I could throw myself on the grass and start eating away like a pasty-skinned, skinny-ass cow.

"Since you can't talk to us, I guess it's best for us to yak once in a while," Trini piped up after a few minutes of silence and stomach gurgling from me and Ridley. Incidentally, two bellies in the throes of starvation? They sounded like quicksand the way movies made quicksand sound like.

And, man, I was starting to sound like Dr. Seuss, but that's hunger for you.

"Dario and I've gained mucho life points from that last fight," Trini continued. "From where we are right now, we can also see Ridley's life points going up, which is totally weird since he's not a character in the game but more like—dunno—like an antibody? That right?"

Ridley turned to me, blinking. "Is she saying that I'm like good virus or helpful bacteria or something like those?" I could only shrug. My brain cells were shot at this point, and I was just going with the flow. And I desperately needed a bag of gummy bears.

"Anyway, we can see the numbers here, but with Eric, we only see him fight and do other things, but that's it. It's almost like he's part of the game as a regular character that doesn't really contribute anything in terms of life points even though it's weird that you're still able to kill monsters."

I rolled my eyes. "Sounds like how it is at my home, actually. Nothing new. Oh, sweet! I can see the castle from here!"

Yep, I sure could! We'd just cleared the last hill and forest, and we were standing in the middle of a colorful meadow with no monsters or generic peasant characters in sight. And there, suddenly appearing in front of us, was Sleeping Possessed-By-Demons Beauty's castle. It was also pretty generic in design, but I was sure that the monsters that waited for us inside weren't anywhere near generic.

It was so weird, standing there, surrounded by 3-D cartoon-like images, including two of our companions. This was probably how it felt like being in a *Twilight Zone* episode—though less cool. Seriously, Rod Serling should've written the game's storyline. Then I wouldn't mind so much getting trapped in it.

"Wait a sec," I said after a moment's silence. I glanced around. "Didn't Althea say that we've got one more ambush before the castle? How's that going to happen?" There was nothing weird anywhere in sight—only miles and miles of fake grass and flowers plus vast expanses of fake blue skies. There weren't CGI animals anywhere, either, but I figured that the demons that cursed the kingdom might've already had all the livestock for lunch.

"We'd better move carefully, then," Ridley said, nodding. His hands immediately glowed, and I noticed that the pulsing light was much, much brighter than it was before. "There's a chance that the ambush can come from the ground—you know, like things crawling out of the earth or something."

"I hear you," I replied, looking down. "This place looks much too pretty and uplifting to make me feel easy."

We moved forward without another word, Dario leading the way as usual. I fidgeted with my knives, my heart thumping, my stomach growling more loudly.

Nothing happened to us as we walked even though we stopped every once in a while to scope out the area and report to each other about possible danger zones. The place was so quiet and brightly colored that I was getting really creeped out. In the meantime, the castle grew larger and larger as we approached, and before I realized it, we were standing in front of its walls, gaping.

The walls were completely covered with thorny rose briars, just like in the fairy tale. And the thorns were massive, probably the same size as a switchblade, and the roses were also gigantic. I didn't know how thick the wall of thorns was, but it looked damned thick, considering the number of skeletons trapped in them.

"Oh, yikes!" I said, grimacing, as I stared at them. "Looks like the game's following the fairy tale, all right. I remember that part about princes and shit getting trapped in the thorns and dying there."

"Ew." Ridley made the same face I made. "Looks like we'll have to cut through them to get inside."

A low hiss suddenly broke through the silence around us, and the skeletons started moving, squirming among the vines as they freed themselves, their bony hands holding up weapons. They slowly hacked their way out of the thorns, hissing and growling as they went.

We all stepped back and looked around. The castle walls all around seemed to have come alive. One by one, skeletons broke out of their prisons and moved toward us. It was like being attacked by an army of the undead—though kind of boring-looking. I'd have settled for ghosts.

And just like that, my stomach growled, and it sounded like it talked and said, "Christ's ass, this sucks!"

Chapter 10

"Watch out!" Ridley yelled, and he stood in front of Dario, raising both hands in front of him. Then here and there, skeletons vanished inside force fields, though a number managed to avoid getting bubbled and came at us, waving their weapons. Whatever spooky silence we had earlier was now filled with groans, hisses, and bones clacking.

"Keep zapping them, Ridley!" I cried out, my voice barely heard above the noise of CGI monsters and the archer's arrows flying through the air.

"I'm trying!" Ridley started running back and forth, "shooting" at oncoming skeletons.

There were so many of them. I didn't think that we'd make it. We were literally being ambushed by dozens and dozens of those things. I guess it made sense, seeing as how a castle was massive, and if its walls were covered with thorns and trapped bodies, being attacked by a big horde wasn't unrealistic. The logic of the situation didn't make it suck any less, though.

Those monsters were harder to pin down. Ridley was red-faced and panting as he tried to zap as many as he could while punching at whatever came close enough for him to kill. Dario fought hard, though I noticed that he had to keep drinking health potions more often than before. He was up against skeletons with massive life point differences from his avatar, so it looked like he'd stop to refuel halfway through each kill. Trini's archer did what she could, also running back and forth, shooting her arrows non-stop, though sometimes she was hacked at by an oncoming skeleton, and she had to run away to drink some health potion.

For my part, I desperately tried to channel Legolas and reminded myself how elves fought with weapons, according to those DVD extras for *The Lord of the Rings*. I should've paid more attention to them, goddamnit. Okay, so I was being a total geek who was in over his head in this game, and there was no way I was going to do battle with an army of insane, demon-possessed skeletons and look like a graceful and kickass elf.

"Oh, what the hell ever!" I snarled, running up to a skeleton. As it stopped and started slicing away at me, I fought as well as I thought I could with two big knives, alternately waving them and aiming for different parts of the skeleton, even managing a few martial arts turns for the hell of it. I mean, come on—I was on fire once I started, and throwing in a few cool moves added to my adrenaline levels.

I also learned how to kick an enemy to force it back in order to rest for a couple of seconds or so, which turned out to be surprisingly helpful. It also moved the monster in the line of the archer's fire, and it took a few hits, staggering toward me with some arrows stuck through its ribs. Pretty cool, actually. I just wished I knew how many life points were being sucked out of it with every arrow finding its way into its fleshless body.

The skeleton I was fighting eventually died, exploding in a gazillion pieces of shattered bone—again very, very *cool*—and leaving a health potion bottle where it stood. I kicked it in the direction of Trini's archer because she was the closest avatar to me. Then I looked around and found Dario's knight getting pummeled by three skeletons at a time.

The avatars were more vulnerable in the game compared to me and Ridley, so I ran toward the knight and planted myself in front of her while she jumped back in order to fish out her health potion and drink. The skeletons she was fighting with turned to me and hacked away.

Man, I wished I weren't so tired and hungry. But I fought as much as I could, given my advantage as a non-killable entity in the game, cutting away at each skeleton that I distracted from Dario's knight. Using those knives worked well since I was able to move quickly and give myself time and momentum to kick a skeleton away, so I could focus on its buddies.

I wasn't sure if it was adrenaline, starvation, or fatigue—or a combination of all three—that made something click, but I suddenly remembered how elves would fight, and I started moving my hands in certain S-shaped and circular patterns. The crazy thing was that once I started doing it, I couldn't stop, and for most of the time I fought that way, my face was frozen in an expression of shock and embarrassment.

"Oh, my God," I panted, turning around to fight the Elvish way, "I'm such a nerd!"

What was even dorkier was the fact that moving my hands and arms as though I were dancing to Madonna's "Vogue" actually saved me some energy. Okay, it might also be my geek side being totally inspired by the whole "channeling Legolas" thing, but in the end, I thought it was seriously *cool*. Embarrassing as all hell, but *cool*. So for the next several moments, I was like a make-believe elf prince kinda-sorta Voguing with a pair of knives, and I was rocking it.

Maybe it was because of the style of fighting, but I was able to cut down those life points with less trouble than before. My weapons managed to find their targets without fail, not like when I was flailing away with that old sword I had, though maybe it was nothing more than Elf-magic at work. I mean, I wouldn't be surprised, seeing as how we were already all geeking out in a game, so how much geekier could it get, infusing some elf elements into the fight?

Whatever. I could barely even understand how this worked out, but I sure as hell was starting to have some fun slaughtering. The only downside to my Ultra Nerd Moment ™ was that I didn't know any Tolkien language, and all I had was "Ha!" or "There!" or "Suck this, asswipe!" instead of something more dignified-sounding from the old Elf-tongue even though I wouldn't know what the hell I was saying.

I was even able to kill one of the three skeletons before Dario's knight returned to finish off the group. I kept looking around for the archer to see if she needed any help, but she looked like she was able to keep herself much safer compared to the knight.

"Keep an eye out for health potions, everyone!" Trini called out.

At this point, it was hard to break away and gather those things, which were popping up all over the place with every skeleton we killed. But at least Ridley and I worked together to give Trini and Dario enough time to claim what they needed and refuel before diving back into the fight.

"Since you're almost as vulnerable as the others, maybe we should switch places here and there," I panted, running up to Ridley and helping him finish off a couple of skeletons with a few seriously stylized Elf moves. "Being up here in the front means taking most of the hits, so maybe I should stay here with Dario since I can't be killed. You can back up Trini and zap away whenever you need to."

Ridley, who was now completely out of breath and beet-red from so much action, could only nod, slap my shoulder, and then run off to join Trini's archer, huffing loudly. Poor guy. I hoped this stupid misadventure in the land of video games meant that he'd have something to show for it when the heroes got together for their usual search-and-rescue practice missions. I remembered Magnifiman nagging him before about his speed in defending people and also his confidence.

I took my place near Dario's knight and kept one eye on her and another on advancing skeletons. Most of them were still hiding inside Ridley's force fields, which really sucked ass, because it meant we were nowhere near finished with those bastards. I hoped that Althea and the Sentries' grand scheme would take effect, like, *right now,* so we could all catch a break.

In between gulping air and coughing, I muttered all kinds of geeky stuff to keep myself going. "Okay—we're up against Orcs. Those über ones, anyway. We're protecting Helm's Deep. Or whatever. No, the ring. Who the fuck's got the ring in this sad group, anyway? Why can't we just get him out of here, so we won't be attacked left and right?"

Here, there, and wherever, went the pair of Elvish knives (though I kind of wished that I had special holsters or something to carry them in and whip them out when needed), and there I was, more and more sure that I looked like I was Voguing to whoever could see me at that moment. S-shaped move here, C-shaped slice there, a duck and a turn, and sometimes a kick thrown in for good measure. I mean—I could be my own hybrid Elvish and martial arts trainer. I guess the only thing missing was Madonna's music, so I could at least use it as a guide for those "special" moves. This was, like, a gay boy's RPG in its most extreme form.

Note to self: beg and plead with the Sentries to use that memory device on everyone—and I mean *everyone*—when this was over because, God, I wouldn't be able to live any of this nerd stuff down. Whatever I felt for Trini and Dario getting their brains zapped to protect the heroes' identities was gone forever. If it meant requiring a lobotomy, so be it. Just—I did *not* want to be reminded of how I kicked monster ass in this Satan's spawn of a game.

The skeleton I was fighting with finally died, and I turned just as it exploded, catching sight of Dario's knight stopping her fight and running off, most likely to drink another health potion. A couple of skeletons went after her, but I ran and planted myself in front of them, forcing them to fight me instead. Gummy bears. Man, I so needed them.

"Althea!" I yelled after offing one skeleton and dropping one knife because my grip had loosened from fatigue and sweat. "Get your butt in here and help us out!"

I dove to the ground and rolled—yep, another kickass move right there—and got the knife, stumbling and then falling back on my bony butt when my knees gave out, though I kept a death grip on my weapons. The skeleton I was fighting followed me, hissing and groaning, a couple of arrows in its rib cage, and raising a pretty nasty-looking sword that looked like it belonged to a pirate ship, not a castle. Maybe that'd be another stupid game planning error type of thing, but I didn't have time to stop and think.

From where I sat like a total loser, I gave up on pretending like I was an Elf-prince and starting swiping awkwardly at the skeleton's kneecaps with my knives. Well, it sure as hell was better than nothing, as long as I was cutting down its life points. It stopped and loomed over me, hacking away at my skull and not showing much for its efforts, though I kept slicing at its knees and calves.

"Man, I'm so tired," I panted, pausing if only to let my arms rest for a moment because they were starting to lock up in their sockets. I dragged a sleeve across my forehead and looked around.

The archer and Ridley were at a bit of a distance from me, and they were busy. The knight had taken her place again, and I saw her toss her sword aside, run, and claim one that appeared when a skeleton she was fighting died. Good for her—it could only mean that Dario had managed to earn enough life points to be able to use an advanced weapon, though I wouldn't be surprised if the damage points were still at the basic level at this point of the game, considering we were still slightly advanced beginners fighting our way to the final stages, if that made any sense.

I went back to slicing away at my enemy's kneecaps till the stupid pile of bones finally exploded, and it was all I could do to drag myself across the ground, find some momentum that way, and force myself to get back up on my feet.

"Sonofabitch," I breathed, drooping, when I saw three skeletons being let out of their force field and coming straight for me. "I don't think I can do this anymore."

Then just as those skeletons were about to swan dive and tackle me, the game froze. I mean, *froze*. Everything stopped moving—well, all of the monsters, anyway. I stood there, bracing myself, my knives at the ready even though

I seriously didn't have any strength left, and I was sure that there was no way in hell that I was going to be able to kill them within our limited time.

"What the..?" I panted, looking around and blinking away the sweat that continued to trickle into my eyes. Nearby, both the knight and the archer were also frozen in mid-battle.

"What happened?" Ridley yelled, turning around where he stood and sweeping his gaze all over.

"I don't know! Everything just stopped!"

He hesitated, looking around some more, and then ran over to me. He looked as crappy as I did. We were both drenched in sweat, barely able to move, and totally red-faced. "This is Althea, I'm sure," he said after waiting for his breathing to slow down, and I nodded.

"Hey, guys!"

Ridley and I quickly whipped around and saw one of the skeletons that was about to come after me talking. Possessed by Spirit Wire, as usual, though in this case, because the game was frozen, it didn't move at all save for its mouth. Or more like exposed teeth and jaws. It was fixed in place, its arm raised, its bony fingers wrapped around the handle of a wicked-looking ax. But its head had turned to face us probably because it was caught in that pose when the game froze.

"Althea! What happened?" I asked, hurrying up to the skeleton. "No, wait—you can't hear me. Damn."

"Actually, I can now. Listen, we can't waste time here. The Sentries and I've managed to freeze the game and lock everything down for now, but we can only do it for no more than thirty minutes."

"That's a long time, really," Ridley said.

"No, it isn't. You have to go in the castle and look for the others. Have you ever been inside a castle, even if it's only make-believe?"

I frowned. "If it's make-believe, that kind of makes the point moot, doesn't it?"

"Okay, whatever. Just trust me when I say that that's not enough time. You have to search the castle and get the others together, so the Sentries and I can lock on to you as a group and get you the hell out of there."

"But what about the game?" I asked. "I mean, I thought we were supposed to finish it in order to get out of it."

"Screw the game. We've already messed with it, and whatever that guy said about finishing the game doesn't apply anymore, but time's still a problem. Go past that, you're stuck in there for good. At this point, we need to make sure that you're all together, so we can pull you out of the game and then destroy it."

Ridley and I looked at each other. "There are only two of us, Althea," I retorted. "Our allies back there are frozen along with the rest of the game. How're we going to find the others without their help?"

"Follow the game, then! Keep moving forward, using the main road or path that you're supposed to take to begin with, and don't stray from it. I can sense the others, and while I don't know where they are exactly in the castle, I can tell that you don't have to move off the main path to find them."

"So they're all okay, then?" I asked.

"I think so," Althea stammered, which wasn't a good sign. "I mean, I can feel them in the castle, but my readings are weird. I know they're in there, but vital signs are—uh—weird."

I looked at Ridley, my freak out levels skyrocketing. "What the hell does that mean? Are they okay, or aren't they?"

"I don't know! They're not dead or injured if that's what you're wondering. Just look for them!"

Easier said than done. How the hell were we going to find three superheroes whose vital signs were "weird"? I didn't even know what Althea meant by that, and it sure took me everything I had to stop myself from marching up to the nearest skeleton and slapping the holy heck out of it till its skull broke off from its body and exploded.

"Okay, so let me get this straight," Ridley piped up. "We've got thirty minutes to find the others, who're inside the castle and pretty much in our, you know, line of vision or whatever, right?"

"Right."

"And are the monsters in the castle just as frozen as everything else out here?"

"Yep, they are, but I can't keep them frozen for too long, and here's one more catch. The moment you find the last person you need to find, the program unfreezes, and you'll be under attack left and right."

"Oh, great," I muttered, grimacing. "This was how my recurring childhood nightmares worked. Put a foot wrong, and all the ghosts and monsters wake up and come after me."

"Dude, the game has to unfreeze in order for me to get you out. There's no other way to do it. So you'd better go. Once you're all together, I'll sense that, and I'll communicate with you again to make sure that you don't wander off, separate, and screw everything up while the game unfreezes. Now go!"

Ridley and I didn't need another push. Without a word exchanged between us, we tore past the army of frozen skeletons. The gates to the castle grounds were partly open at that point, which most likely happened when the skeletons came alive. The big-ass rose briars were also gone, leaving the walls bare. But there were so many skeletons scattered all over, over half of them still inside force field bubbles. My skin crawled at the thought of those things coming alive to swarm the castle if we didn't make it.

"Thirty minutes!" I cried as we ran through a massive open court thing that was also littered with frozen ghouls. "How're we going to find them in thirty minutes?"

"God, I don't know!" Ridley said, sounding desperate. "I'm too tired to run fast enough!"

I wanted to stop and look at the monsters surrounding us more closely, but no way in hell was I going to be caught in that place with swarms of undead creatures coming after me once our time ran out. Whatever glimpses I had as I followed Ridley along a path of stone that was clearly marked for us—the stones were colored a light gray compared to the dark and blood-spattered, grimy floors of the rest of the courtyard—showed things that were the stuff of nightmares. They were all corpses lying asleep, just as it was in the fairy tale (save for the corpse part), and I figured that being alive and warm-blooded would break the spell, and all of those horrible things would wake up. They'd be something like zombies, for sure, but they gave me the worst case of the willies compared to that other zombie attack we had. From what I managed to see, they looked way too realistic and horrifying as dead people in the same way that the undead in my nightmares were realistic.

We barreled through the main doors that led inside the castle. Man, it felt like we were trapped inside an amusement park haunted house thing. If it came with a ride like the one in Disney's "Haunted Mansion" deal, that'd be great, but we were stuck depending on our feet and our energy levels.

The castle was dark with only a few torches lighting up our way. What was freakier was the fact that our path toward the final destination, the tower room where Sleeping Possessed Beauty lay, was nothing more than a narrow, dark corridor lined with torches and an occasional sleeping dead person. Some of the corpses even lay right in our path, so we had to step over them, freaking out and shivering. I felt as though I'd reverted to being five years old, when I was convinced that stepping over a dead body in my dreams meant having that corpse come alive just as I put one foot over it, and it'd reach out and grab my ankle with its cold, dry hand.

Our vision was also limited to maybe fifty feet ahead because nothing but shadows filled the area beyond that point. So every step forward meant an element of surprise for us, and I seriously was over surprises at that point.

"Ow. Dude, ow."

"Huh?"

"You're cutting off my circulation. Quit with the death grip."

I blinked and looked down. Somehow I'd managed to grab hold of Ridley's right arm with my left hand, fusing my stiff fingers around it like steel claws. I held on to my knives with my right hand, which also kept a death grip on them.

"Sorry. This is like reliving a recurring nightmare I had when I was a kid," I said, letting Ridley go and barely taking notice of him massaging that part of his arm that I'd probably damaged. "I never thought I'd be so freaked over a game, but I am. Any idea how much therapy is? I hope my parents have me covered under their insurance."

"Don't know, but I'm sure we'll end up seeing the same doctor. Maybe there's such a thing as a group discount."

The temperature inside the castle wasn't cold, but the smell was weird. It was old, musty, and moldy, which didn't solve my extreme paranoia problem. What was worse was that my imagination was starting to go into overdrive, and I could've sworn that some of those corpses we passed moved a little. I swallowed and glanced back to make sure we weren't followed. The corridor behind us was quiet but no less creepy. I still couldn't help but sense that we weren't the only ones in the castle who were up and about, and the only good thing about this was that at least the air didn't reek of rotting corpses.

The corridor turned sharp corners, and those were hairy moments. More than once, we turned a super dark corner, only to come face-to-face with a corpse that wasn't lying down but was sleeping on its feet while leaning against the wall, its head turned as though it were waiting for us to show up. Whenever we spotted one of those, we both had to stop, freak out for a couple of seconds, and then move forward, pressing ourselves against the opposite wall to avoid coming within two feet of the sleeping corpse thing.

"I don't see Peter and the others anywhere," I hissed after a while. I also realized then that our footsteps echoed in the corridor—or at least they'd begun to, anyway. Maybe we were way deep inside the bowels of the castle at that point, and every little bit of sound bounced off walls and stuff. "Do you?"

Ridley shook his head. I heard him swallow. "Nope. Just corpses that make me want to give up gaming for the rest of my life and beyond."

"God, they're supposed to be turned into things that blend in with the scenery. What if they were turned into one of these corpses?"

"I don't know," Ridley stammered. "Something tells me that they weren't. Gut feeling. I've learned to trust that."

"I hope you're right. This castle's packed with sleeping dead bodies, and it'll be hell trying to find the others if they've been turned into one of those gross things."

The longer we walked and searched, the more unsettling the place became. With the echoes filling the silence with distorted sounds, I couldn't help but sense that we weren't alone. Or at least we weren't the only ones who were awake and moving around, and that feeling grew stronger and stronger as we moved along. Ridley stayed in front, his hands nothing more than a pair of glowing balls, while I stayed as close as I could behind him, my grip on my knives alternately tightening and loosening as I kept looking behind me with every strange echo I heard.

As usual, I saw nothing but sleeping corpses, an occasional torch, and solid blackness beyond a fifty-foot distance. I suppose I should be grateful that we had that fifty-foot leeway should the corpses suddenly come alive and chase after us, but I didn't feel particularly thankful for anything at that moment.

Ridley and I made a couple more turns and then found ourselves stepping through a big open door and staring, drop-jawed, at what looked like a throne room. It was massive, like it could hold a hundred or so people with lots of extra room to move around in. It was lit—kind of dimly, though—with several torches along the walls, and hanging from the ceiling were old and torn up pennants. If anything, there seemed to be way more cobwebs than pennants above us. The thrones for both king and queen stood on a dais that was set against the opposite end of where we entered, and there sat both monarchs. Oh, yeah, they were also totally dead, their bodies slumped in their thrones, their arms hanging off the sides, their heads bowed. And scattered all over the area were dozens of the same old, same old nightmarish bodies, every one of them looking like they hadn't gone through a process of mummification yet because their skin appeared soft and full though discolored, not dry and hard and sinking against bone. Their eyes were either closed and practically fused shut or partly open, so that we could see their dried up eyeballs through the dusty gaps. Their bodies' positions also looked stiff, which was understandable if they died lying on the floor like that. They all looked like the bodies of people who'd recently died.

Oh, and have I mentioned the echoes? Yeah, there were echoes in that throne room, and I'm not just talking about the sounds that Ridley and I made, walking, talking in whispers, and constricting our bladders to keep them from messing up our underwear. There were other softer, weirder sounds that seemed to come from nowhere.

"Ridley, wait," I whispered, stopping and listening, holding my breath. Ridley froze and looked back at me.

"What's wrong?"

"Ssshh. Listen."

We both fell silent and strained our ears. I sure as hell had no idea what kinds of sound effects were created for a game like this one, but it seemed as though what sounded like footsteps from some distance as well as faint, hollow voices were a part of the program. The footsteps—or what sounded like footsteps—were irregular, like someone walking for a few paces and then stopping before taking a couple more steps and then stopping again, etc. The voices were the ones that really upped the creepy meter for me because they sounded more like sighs or light giggling, but I couldn't tell for sure. I knew that they were voices, but whether or not they were forming words was hard to distinguish. All I was aware of at that moment was my hair standing on end and my skin breaking out in goosebumps.

"We gotta get out of here," I whispered again. "I can't stand this anymore."

Ridley looked back at the throne room. "Do you think they're in here?"

"We don't have a choice but to look," I replied. "We just have to be quick about it. I can see a door over there by that corner. I think that's our way out of here."

With that, we both hurried forward, staying as close together as we possibly could, looking over the corpses, focusing our search in the center of the throne room first before moving along the perimeter, checking the bodies lying near or against the walls as well as the thrones. I don't think my hair went down the whole time. It felt like I'd doused myself with extra hold hairspray, and every hair up and down my body was standing at attention. Seriously, things looked way, way different from the other end of a computer game, and I was sure that I wouldn't be hyperventilating in terror if my view of the castle and corpses were limited to computer animation that I could control with the use of a mouse and a keyboard.

"God, I'll never, *ever* play another computer game again other than retro Pac-Man," I muttered as I shadowed Ridley, subjecting myself to more of the same kind of psychological trauma that'd make shrinks tons of money. Our footsteps sounded loud and harsh against my ears, and so did my breathing. I tried to ignore those other sounds, but I couldn't. Those damned voices got under my skin, and I couldn't shake them off so easily. I didn't know if Ridley was able to, and it was hard to guess what was going through his mind as he had his superhero face on.

"They're not all here," Ridley said after another moment, and we stopped, looking around. "But—it's weird, Eric, but I feel that one of them is. I mean, here—in this room with us."

I stared at him. "You can sense the others the way Althea can?"

He shrugged, looking a little helpless and confused. "I think so. I mean—maybe that's because of my leveling up from all those life points I earned, or maybe it's because of genetics. I don't know. I just—all I'm sure about now is that one of the others is in this room right now." His voice grew louder and surer. He nodded as he looked around. "Yeah, I'm sure of it now. The feeling's strong."

"But I didn't see anyone—only dead bodies that're set to wake up any minute now, and no one looked familiar," I said, and if I didn't had knives on me, I'd be wringing my hands in desperation.

"No, no—it's different. I mean, what I sense is different. I think…" Ridley's voice faded, and he fell silent for a few seconds, frowning as he thought things over. "If one of them is here, then he or she is transformed but not in the way that's obvious in the game. I sensed that no one's been turned into a corpse, but if they're supposed to blend in with the scenery…" His words faded.

I frowned. I even almost scratched my head, but I quickly realized that I was holding a knife in each hand and was relieved that I caught that before I could scalp myself and create even more scenarios of absolute horror. "You mean he or she's in superhero form? I didn't see anyone in spandex anywhere. Or in Freddie's case, I didn't see any dorky-looking Japanese monster rubbing elbows with dead people." Then I stopped and pinched my eyes shut. "Oh, I'm such a dumbass. They're supposed to blend in with the scenery. That's right—I keep ignoring that bit."

"It's simple, and it makes sense," Ridley said, and he walked toward the nearest wall, staring long and hard at it. "And I think I understand what Althea meant when she said their vital signs seem weird."

"Okay, so they've been turned into objects that are a part of the castle. Like hell are we gonna be able to find them in time. That's just as bad as all of them turning into corpses and mixing it up with the rest of the bodies here."

"No, wait—it'll be okay. I'm sure of it."

He talked slowly, the way people talked whenever they were speaking out their thoughts as ideas trickled through. Then he started to walk around the throne room again, his eyes riveted to the walls, and it was all I could do to follow him, praying under my breath that we weren't wasting too much time in that room. I kept glancing around to make sure that we were the only ones moving.

Ridley suddenly stopped. "Wade's here," he said, his voice firmer but still in a whisper. Then he looked at me, grinning. "I can sense her. Or more like I spotted her." He raised a hand, the glowing bubble around it vanishing, and he pointed at the wall directly across from us. "See? She's been transformed according to her powers, it looks like."

I stared long and hard at the wall and at first saw nothing but a line of torches. Then it dawned on me. One of the torches looked different. Its fire was brighter, more vivid, almost cartoon-like in the way it glowed starkly against the dark walls, while the other torches lit the throne room with dull, yellow fire.

"One of these things is not like the others," I said, returning Ridley's grin. I lost no time and quickly tiptoed through the scattered corpses to the opposite wall.

The torch we were looking at was set on a holder of some kind, and it was easy for me to pull it out. The torch itself was made of something like smooth metal that was a bright red shade, which mimicked Wade's superhero costume as Miss Pyro. The rest of the torches were made of the usual dark brown wood that looked old and rotten.

"Okay, let's get out of here," Ridley said, and he led me through the door that we spotted earlier.

It took us into another corridor that wasn't any different from the one we were in. Narrow, dark, and occasionally littered with corpses, it made the throne room feel like a quick break in between claustrophobia-laced nightmares. The only comfort I had at that point was having Wade with us even though she wasn't exactly going to be helpful in any fight that was set to break out soon. What she did, though, was light up the corridor like a Fourth of July fireworks display when I held her up. It was as though her fire—or maybe fire power—was on full blast, and in torch form, she cut down on the trauma by not only lighting up our immediate space with super brightness, but also blast the shadows beyond fifty feet, so that we could see well past that. I was never a good judge when it came to distance, but I was sure that her fire power helped us see clearly all the way to a hundred feet either ahead of us or behind us.

For a moment, I wondered if Wade used to be a lighthouse in a past life. I mean, you know—these things could get complicated and bizarre.

"Wade," I said, panting, as we ran through the nightmarish maze, "I hope you can still somehow use your offense powers even while transformed like this. I swear I won't abuse them, but when push comes to shove, I'll really, really need your help."

Naturally, Wade couldn't answer, though the fire seemed to hiccough a couple of times, showering us with some harmless sparks the same way wood in a fireplace or campfire would pop and shower sparks. I felt my terror levels lower then, and seeing Ridley's fists once again glowing with his own defense powers made me feel even better and more protected.

Of course, one thought kept crossing my mind the whole time—what forms would Freddie and Peter take if they were both changed like Wade? Freddie could be anything! If we were inside a game about a fairy tale, I figured that he'd be changed into something that had to work with the setting somehow, which meant no dorky Japanese monsters anywhere. I mean, sure, it would've been great if he'd somehow turned into a miniaturized Godzilla, as it'd be easy to spot him and even use him as part of our arsenal against corpses coming to life. But in a classic fairy tale setting, I couldn't even begin to imagine what form he'd take.

I grimaced. Come to think of it, what the hell form would Peter take? He had speed and super strength powers, which translated to what?

"Well, at least I don't need to pee," I muttered, glancing behind me when I thought I heard those creepy, hollow voices ringing along the corridor.

Chapter 11

After what felt like an eternity, we found ourselves inside another big room, which turned out to be a banquet room. It was as huge as the throne room, and this time, we saw long tables that ran along three of four sides in a U-shape thing. The tables were covered with old, tattered, and soiled tablecloths, and the food and plates sitting on them were rotten, moldy, and buried under thick cobwebs.

As for the people who were struck down during a feast—well, they were all slumped in their chairs, looking no different from the other corpses we'd seen so far. The walls were again lined with torches, though nothing stood out this time, which meant that we were carrying around the correct torch to save from this game.

"Do you feel anything?" I asked Ridley as I followed him around the room, looking at the corpses to make sure that neither Freddie nor Peter was hobnobbing it with those nasty things. Thankfully they weren't.

"I do, yeah. But I don't see anything out of place here." Ridley stopped after we made our first round. "Maybe we should split up and look again."

I stared at him, trying not to panic. "Okay, I'll buy the argument that splitting up will save us time, but if something moves and comes after us, I'm going to lose it, and not only am I going to blame you, but I'm taking you down with me."

"Nothing's going to happen until we find all three of them," Ridley said, though he looked as freaked as I felt. Both of us kept looking around furtively, making sure that we were still the only ones moving. This game was turning us into a pair of obsessive-compulsive types. "We can't avoid that. The only thing we can do now is to make it happen as quickly as possible. Dude, we gotta get this over with."

"I know, I know. Still doesn't make it any less sucky."

Ridley patted my shoulder and walked off. At least he left me with Wade. She might not be much help at the moment beyond giving me a lot of light, but knowing that she was with me helped temper my panic, especially since those weird echoes were back. My skin kept crawling, and I kept gulping in deep breaths to counter that feeling.

Ridley and I went opposite ways, with him going clockwise around the room, and me going counterclockwise. I held up Wade the Magic Torch and used one knife to poke around some of the bodies and dishes. I couldn't see anything out of place, and I was about to meet Ridley midway through.

"Shit," I said, stopping and looking around again. "Where is he?" I thought I heard a thin, metallic voice laugh from some far corner of the castle, and I shuddered again.

I was about to take another step forward when I spotted it. Him. It. Whatever. It was like part of a suit of armor sitting on the floor and leaning against the wall. Just like Wade the Magic Torch before, this one—Freddie or Peter—stood out starkly against the godawful setting. The armor was more like just the upper half that covered the torso, made up of the front and back plates with something like leather straps on the sides that needed to be buckled together in order to hold everything in place. The plates were nicely decorated with patterns that looked Medieval or fairy tale-ish, I guess, and they were also polished to a high sheen. Yep. Looked like we found our guy. Thing. Whatever.

"Now who the hell would this be?" I asked, frowning. Then I called out to Ridley. "I found him! Don't know who this is, but he got turned into armor!"

"Huh? Seriously?" Ridley ran up to me, looking confused. For a moment we stood there, staring blankly at the armor pieces. "Wow. I—uh—I don't know what to say."

"So who's going to wear him?" I asked. "I can't believe I just asked that. That sounded totally wrong, didn't it? It's like talking about wearing someone's skin."

"I've got my suit on, so you'll have to do it."

"You're kidding."

"Nope. And you'd better put him on quick before we run out of time."

I stared at Ridley for a moment. "You do realize that the longer I participate in this game and do weird stuff like this, the greater my chance of growing up to be a psychopath."

"That's what therapists are for. Come on, put him on. Here. Lemme hold Wade." Ridley blushed when he reached out a hand and took the torch from me. "That didn't sound right, either, did it? Sorry Wade," he said, turning to talk to the torch in his hand. "I wasn't sexually harassing you."

The flames shot up once, again punctuating that with another shower of sparks. Wade must've just given Ridley the middle finger. In the meantime, I quickly put the armor on, which proved to be an awkward process. The front and back plates were—duh!—stiff and cold, and I fumbled with the leather straps on the sides, my hands all shaking and sweaty as I tried to get things done as quickly as possible. It felt so big and bulky and crazy awkward. Not to mention seriously embarrassing.

"Okay, I'm set," I said, glancing up and meeting Ridley's baffled stare. "I know, I look like a monumental loser wearing this. I don't even know who this happens to be."

"I think it's Freddie," Ridley said, handing the torch back to me. "I mean, it makes sense, right? He's the shapeshifter of the bunch, and he sometimes takes on robot masks or masks that involve guns or anything metallic for defense and offense."

"Yeah, I see what you mean," I replied, holding on to the torch. "Which leaves us with Peter. And that's really messing with my mind because if he's going to be transformed, I don't even know what I can associate him with. I mean—he's all about speed and strength. What the hell would that make him?"

"We'll find out soon enough. Maybe you should leave your knives behind since you might not need them anymore."

"What—are you kidding? We're going to get ambushed! I need something to use!" Then Wade the Magic Torch spluttered again, and I frowned at her. It. Whatever. "Wade, if you're trying to tell me to trust you, it's kind of hard to do that, seeing as how you're not exactly a weapon I can use."

Ridley sighed. "Come on, dude, let's go. Don't worry about the knives. I think we'll be okay. Remember nothing here can hurt any of us, anyway—"

"No, but things can still hold us back and eat up our time," I retorted, but at this point, I'd already dropped my knives and was running out another door, following Ridley as he tore down one more corridor. I guess, to some extent, I did feel more soothed by the fact that I had both Wade and Freddie with me, with Freddie literally protecting me from harm even though defense wasn't really necessary. Then again, it also helped not having to carry him in one hand the way I was carrying Wade, though with him as armor that I wore, I felt like a sad little nerd neck-deep in RPG.

"By the way, Freddie," I said, stealing a glance down at the armor vest thingie I wore, "don't get any ideas. Having you wrapped around me like this will probably be your first taste of gayness, but that's all you'll be getting from me."

I didn't know how many more corners we turned, with those creepy-ass sounds following us wherever we went, but eventually we ended up standing in a foyer-type room with massive double doors opposite us. Corpses were strewn all over the floor.

"God, we're, like, running deeper and deeper inside this castle without any break," Ridley said with a tired sigh. "Come on, let's go." Picking his way carefully through the corpses, he led me to the doors and pushed them open without trouble. "Oh, yay!"

I hurried after him and found that we'd reached an open courtyard. It was massive, easily about five times the size of the throne room (maybe more), but it was still a part of the castle, and the castle's second half—or whatever it was called—stood a good distance before us, and I figured that that was where the tower room lay. Then again, the tower room wasn't our problem anymore, according to Althea. To our right and left were the castle's battlements, standing around the height of a three-storey apartment building. There was no gate or doorway on either side, which meant that we had to enter the second half of the castle in order to get out.

Which, by the way, sucked massively, but that wasn't all.

In between the open area where we stood and the castle's second half stretched a garden maze type of thing, made of super tall shrubbery that was all dead and rotting. Since the maze was so ginormous and appeared to fuse itself to the battlements—read: there was no room around that'd allow us to bypass it—it was obvious that the only way to the second half of the castle was to find our path through the maze.

Great. Another obstacle course to suffer through under time pressure. And we still had to find Peter.

The area was, like the castle, dotted with corpses lying on the stone floor, which was cracked in several places, with weeds sprouting through. At the sight of those bodies and then the maze, I couldn't help but droop.

"Oh, man, I don't believe this," I said. "There's no way we're going to get out of here in time."

Ridley didn't answer. He stood in place, turning his head, his face slightly tilted up as though he were sniffing the air or watching something above us. "Wait," he said after a moment. "Peter's here. I can sense him."

"Thank God!" I cried, whipping around to scan the area. I raised up Wade, breaking up the shadows around me as I searched the corpses. "I have absolutely no idea what form he'd take, though."

Ridley had walked off to cover the left half of the courtyard. "I don't, either, but whatever it is, it's got to be something that's related to his powers."

"Which leaves me nothing to go by." I sighed as I looked around, half-anxious and half-excited about the fact that we were close to finishing this insane game. I stepped over bodies, still shivering at how awful they all looked, but at least I wasn't in danger of puking where I stood. Every once in a while, though, something would make me stop, gasp, and look up. Since we were outdoors, those weird echoes inside the castle weren't heard, but the creepy feeling of being followed or not being alone remained, and I was no less jumpy than I was indoors.

I swear—I *swear*—some of those corpses moved a little, but when I turned to stare at them, they lay still.

I didn't know how long it was taking us to find Peter, but the awful realization that our time was running out grew starker and starker in my head. Panic started to grow again, and not even having Wade and Freddie there with me helped. I didn't have my knives. I felt horribly vulnerable to anything that'd attack me. Even though I wasn't going to be earning any points, it still meant running the risk of going over our time limit and finding ourselves forever trapped in that freaky castle, perpetually fighting off corpses till—what? Till we collapsed in exhaustion and died? Starvation and thirst would certainly a major issue. God, what a way to go.

I whirled around, gasping, when I thought I saw more movement from the corner of my eye. I held Wade up and looked but saw nothing. A light breeze had picked up, disturbing some of the smaller debris on the floor. I looked at Wade the Magic Torch and was relieved to find her fire not getting disturbed by the movement of air around us.

"Peter!" I called out. I would've whispered, but at that point, I just wanted to find him, pronto, fight off rampaging corpses, and then get my ass saved by Althea within the next ten seconds. "Peter, I know you can hear me!" Wade the

Magic Torch spewed a few sparks. Maybe she was trying to call out to Peter in her own way, too. Kind of cute, really, and I would've appreciated that more if I weren't borderline meltdown-ish.

"If he can, he can't talk back!" Ridley replied from another end of the courtyard, where he was poking around.

"Hey, that pizza promise you made before we got sucked into this game had better be good still," I said. "There ain't no way I'm going to suffer through nightmares every day for the next year without being properly compensated for my trauma."

"Seriously, considering what we've been through? I'm making my parents pay for twice the number of pizzas I promised. But that'll happen right before they ground me for a week or something after they find out about this."

"*If* they find out, you mean. Dude, come on. Get with the program." That said, double the number of pizzas for emotional and psychological compensation? Ridley Russell was now my newest, greatest BFF.

I yelped, leaped over a corpse, and quickly turned around to stare in shock at a pile of bodies I walked past. My heart at this point felt like it had pumped its way up my throat. I could've sworn my Adam's apple was getting forced up my tongue. "Oh, God," I whispered, staring hard at those bodies. "They moved. I know they did."

But with Wade's sunlight-like brightness on them, I saw nothing. In the shadows, though, I thought I saw them move. Okay, this was getting out of hand. The breeze had also gotten a bit stronger.

"Peter!" I yelled even more loudly now. "Goddamnit, where are you?" Again, Wade spewed a few more sparks, which all vanished with the wind currents.

"I can't see him anywhere!" Ridley cried. He'd searched his side of the courtyard and was looking at the maze. "Oh, man, don't tell me he's in the maze somewhere. It'll take us forever to find him."

"Peter! Peter!" I stumbled back to the middle of the courtyard, spinning around in one place as I held Wade up. The wind seemed to have settled on a bearable speed so that Ridley and I could still hear each other and other possible creepy noises as well. And to echo the game world's climate or atmosphere or whatever, the wind felt comfy and not at all cold. It was almost like a summer breeze kind of thing, and even though I was in near-panic mode, I felt comforted by it.

Then Wade spat out a few more sparks, and I froze, shocked. "What—oh, my God—Peter?" I blinked and looked up, searching the sky, even though I knew it was dumb. Who could see the wind, anyway?

Sure enough, I felt something brush against my cheeks. It felt like a soft touch of someone's hand. It also felt like a quick kiss.

"Peter? We found you, didn't we?" I asked quietly now, and I smiled when I felt another light brush of air against my cheeks. How could I be so stupid? Peter's speed and strength—of course, they could be translated into wind!

Wade sent out another shower of sparks. I rolled my eyes when I realized that she might've been trying to tell me something about Peter. I looked at her even though I was in danger of blinding myself by staring right at her super bright fire.

"I think I just figured out what you've been trying to do," I said. "Thanks, girl. I owe you one." I turned to Ridley. "We found Peter! He's been turned into the wind!"

Ridley stood there, looking as though he hadn't heard me. His face was frozen in an expression of absolute horror, his complexion drained of blood, his eyes wide, and his mouth hanging. I could smell total fear rushing out of him from where I stood, maybe about thirty feet away. His gaze was also fixed on something behind me, which was never, ever a good thing.

I turned around and nearly pissed my pants.

Corpses were rising all around us. And it wasn't like they were suddenly awake and conscious and were stumbling to their feet. Hell, no—they were still deader than dead, their eyes either closed still or partly open, the skin around them sunken, their mouths closed or slightly open. When they "rose," they didn't move any body parts. It was like something—an invisible force—was pulling them up from where they lay, so that their bodies lifted up till they all stood on lifeless legs, though they didn't tip over. Whatever invisible force raised them up from the floor kept them upright but drooping.

Then they started moving toward us. They didn't walk, nope. They were moved forward, their feet visibly dragging across the cement, and they looked like lifeless mannequins. Yeah, like real corpses being manipulated to move physically without giving them life. We weren't being ambushed by zombies this time. We were about to be chased by corpses. As far as what they could do to us when they caught us? I wasn't about to hang around long enough to find out.

"Run!" I cried, turning and barreling past Ridley and into the maze. Oddly, the only thing that flashed across my mind at that moment was how much a shrink would cost Mom and Dad.

Ridley was behind me this time, and even with the rush of noise around me—more like noise made up of my screeching and cussing—I heard him shoot at the advancing army of corpses with one loud BLOOMP! after another. I also felt Freddie the Magic Armor tighten around me (seriously, he'd better not be making a pass), while Peter the Magic Wind swirled and Wade the Magic Torch shot out flames. For a moment, I wondered what the hell Peter and Wade were supposed to do till gut instinct told me to leave Peter alone and to use Wade as a weapon of some kind in case we came across corpses in the maze.

"Althea! We're together!" Ridley yelled. "Get us out of here!"

"I don't know how to get out of this maze!" I said, panting, when I skidded to a halt at a dead end. "Shit! Go back! Go back!"

"You go! I'll take up the rear!"

I squeezed past Ridley and followed another path. This one was short, stopping quickly for a sharp turn right, and as I rounded the corner, I had to dig my heels in with a cry. A small group of corpses were directly ahead of us, blocking the way and slowly moving closer.

"Oh, God, they're gross!" I spat out. Sparks flew out from Wade, and my gut once again made me snap back. Gripping the torch more firmly, I swung it down like a weapon—a sword—and a long tendril of fire shot out, snapping in the air. I recognized it as Wade's fire whip, and I swung the torch again, and this time the whip cracked against the corpses, setting them on fire.

They stopped dead—no pun intended—and completely disappeared under bright white flames. The surrounding shriveled up hedges that marked the maze sparked and ignited.

"Crap, I hope I didn't just trap us here with the burning bush," I said, gulping.

But whatever fire power Wade had seemed strong enough to completely obliterate those corpses within seconds, and before long we were staring at a pile of ashes on the ground, with a few flickering flames here and there. The hedges continued to burn, but the fires had died down a bit, so that they were as small as the residual flames on the ground.

"Hurry! Run!"

I didn't need another prodding from Ridley. With a squawk, I leaped over the pile of ashes, feeling the heat of Wade's fire power surround me for a second before vanishing as we continued to barrel through the maze. I kept running into dead ends, and it was like acting out a skit from *The Three Stooges* for us when that happened. Ridley would run into me, we'd tangle in a mass of flailing arms, yelling and panicking, and then I'd free myself and run back to take another path.

Another group of corpses met us when we turned a corner. This time around, they were closer than the other group, and Ridley and I had to turn tail and scramble back, both yelling out our grossed-out-ness, and if I weren't armed with Wade the Magic Torch, I'd be flailing my arms wildly the way Ridley was.

We stopped after retreating several feet, and I had to turn around and subject myself to more nightmare material, again using Wade for offense and defense. Since those disgusting moving dead bodies were closer in range, something told me that I couldn't use the fire whip, so I lowered the torch and aimed it at the advancing group.

Wade's fire swelled up, almost went supernova, and then it blasted the group with large fire bombs. The corpses stopped when they were consumed by fire, and I swore I could hear weird voices coming from them—like dull moans or something like that—as they quickly burned to ashes. Were they the same voices I heard earlier inside the castle? Maybe. Those earlier ones might've easily been my overactive imagination going crazy, but who knows?

"Ridley, how're you doing with your force fields?" I asked, barely glancing back as I waited for the right moment to charge forward.

"I'm able to hold them back. We passed a few paths back there, too, where corpses came out to follow us, but I got them. Peter's also tearing down the maze behind us by blowing down hedges and shit and making a mess of the paths. He's keeping those corpses out or at least slowing them down." Ridley sounded out of breath as well as tight with sky-high anxiety. "God, I wish Althea would hurry!"

I felt the breeze around us again, calming me with those familiar touches against my face. "We'll be okay," I whispered, managing to crack a small smile. "Let's go!"

I ran forward, leaped, and tore down the path. The process repeated with more and more frequency because it looked like the closer we got the center of the maze, the more corpses we ran across. Exhaustion was unbearable. I was so sore and hungry and totally, totally zapped of energy, but we had to keep on moving while Althea did whatever the hell she needed to do to get us out.

"Althea! Now would be a really nice time to get out!" I yelled while blasting at two groups of corpses that came out of two intersecting paths. "I'm sure Wade and Peter are losing energy!"

"Don't forget me!" Ridley snapped.

"Oh, and Ridley, too!"

I led Ridley down a path, which mercifully didn't have any corpses. Panting, I didn't let up as I ran, and I hoped that we'd be safe for a little bit longer as I noticed that Wade's fire flickered a lot. I guessed that she was as tired as everyone else was—probably more so since she was doing all of the offensive work without help, while Peter and Ridley took care of the rear and protected us.

The pathway ended, and we stumbled into an open area. It was the center of the maze, judging from all the other paths terminating there from all directions.

"Oh, great," I hissed, turning around and around. "Which path do we take?"

"None," Ridley said, and I heard him gulp. "They're all blocked."

Sure enough, from every open path that linked to the maze's center, corpses appeared, slipping past the entryways and slowly moving toward us. The path that we'd just taken was blocked off as well, as Peter had torn down parts of the hedges behind us.

I looked at Ridley. "I'll see you at the shrink's office in a week." Sad part was that Ridley nodded in agreement.

Chapter 12

"On the count of three," Ridley said as we stood close to each other. "One, two, three!"

We started blasting corpses randomly considering how many there were coming after us, and we moved around in a never-ending circle. Here and there, corpses were either swallowed up by force fields or small fireballs, the latter making me think that Wade was probably at the lowest point of her energy levels. Either that or shooting out small fireballs was her way of using a sub-machine gun. Whatever the reason, it helped by and large, though the damage quotient appeared to be less than her fire whip and those bigger fire bombs. Those corpses that managed to slip past Wade and Ridley's arsenal got kicked back by the winds. At least it looked that way. I mean, they'd be advancing slowly, their stiff feet dragging across the stone ground, and then, BAM! There'd be this rush of strong wind screaming down at them, and they'd suddenly fly backward as though they'd been punched with a wrecking ball, knocking down whatever was in their wake. They looked like a bunch of nasty-ass bowling pins flying all over the place.

"Althea!" I screamed when I noticed Wade's flames sputter more and more. "Get us out of here!"

Since I was stupid enough to listen to Ridley and leave my knives behind, I frantically looked for weapons whenever corpses were killed. I spotted a smallish sword lying a few feet away, and I abandoned Ridley for a moment to claim it, aiming the torch at three corpses that were in my way and blasting them with fire. Once I had the sword in hand, I rushed back to stand as close as I could to him.

"Wade, you've done your job," I said. "Take it easy now. Let me fight them off while I still can." Wade the Magic Torch sputtered and then calmed down, her fire looking smaller and less bright than before. Yeah, she was seriously tired.

I swallowed and tightened my hold on the sword, hoping that my sweaty hand wasn't going to mess things up for me. When the nearest corpses came close enough, I charged forward and swung, slashing at them again and again and cutting down on their life points. Since they were obviously so advanced compared to me and my own life points relative to this stage in the game, they didn't go down at all, but at least I was able to reduce those points somewhat to make it easy for Peter to swoop around me and blast them away with wind power, sending them somersaulting off. Then I focused on the next few corpses that came close. As it usually happened in a game: shampoo, rinse, repeat.

I guess it helped that I was practically insane from terror and revulsion that I never let any of them touch me. Seeing them up close was enough to crank up the violence meter past the stratosphere, which powered me all the way through.

Every once in a while, I saw Ridley charging forward as well to use his power punches, which Peter also supplemented with his own version of hand-to-hand, throwing damaged corpses back, which I was sure ate at their life points even more. My arms were screaming. My left hand held up Wade, and I could only use my right hand to fight with the sword. My weapon might be small, but it wasn't as easy to use as those knives. If I could, I'd use both hands, but there was no way in hell I was going to let Wade go.

I wasn't sure if it was nothing more than a half-crazed brain that made me see something flash from the corner of my eye, but something did. I turned and saw nothing but corpses either getting blasted away or disappearing under another force field. I shook my head and hacked again.

"What in heck?" There it was again! I blinked and looked, and sure enough, it happened for real.

A flash of light—the way light poured through a crack. Was that Althea trying to break in? I almost fainted from joy when another flash broke through the shadows and mayhem in another part of the courtyard.

"It's Althea!" Ridley cried, sounding excited. "She's trying to get through!"

I let out a whoop of joy and used that to feed my aching muscles for a bit longer. I didn't realize it till then that I was stepping closer and closer toward Ridley and that it was the force of the wind that gently pushed me back while I fought, or at least whenever I stepped away. Peter, it looked like, was trying to get us all together in one group. Before I knew it, Ridley and I were standing back to back, and I could feel something like a solid wall of rushing air spinning around us.

More light broke through the scene around us, and this time, the cracks were several. Small ones, large ones, on the ground, the air, the sky—they kept tearing up the scene. It was bizarre, seeing physical, jagged cracks appearing in mid-air or even cutting across a small group of corpses as they were nothing more than a part of a painted scenery. Then the lights flashed more and more quickly, the cracks spreading and expanding, till it looked as though we were about to get swallowed up in brightness.

"Ridley!" I yelled, pinching my eyes shut as we were suddenly flooded with blinding whiteness, and I felt myself pressed hard against Ridley's back by Peter as the wind literally tightened around us.

I heard Ridley yell when the brightness gave way to a sudden, sharp feeling of being snapped back through space as though we were both at the end of a bungee cord. As a group, bundled together by Peter in wind form, we tumbled through light and color and warmth, howling till our voices cracked.

Then the light vanished, the spinning stopped, and we hit the ground in a mass, tumbling, sliding, rolling, and tangled up. Then, BAM! We all slammed against something big and super hard, and we all yelped in pain, though we finally stopped moving.

I didn't know how long it took my brain to stop whirling around in my skull, but I sure as hell was dizzy for a while. I figured that the others were, too, because no one moved for what felt like a billion years, and we just lay there in a crumpled, twisted heap, all groaning and cussing.

"Wow," someone said from what sounded like a major distance. Eventually the ringing in my ears stopped, and I recognized Brenda's voice. "That's a gnarly game of Twister you guys are playing."

"I took a picture. I'll email it to everyone." That one was Althea, by the way. Bitch.

I finally managed to crack my eyes open, and what I managed to see through my glasses—which rested cockeyed on my face—was something that could easily be turned into a horror movie involving teenagers and gore. Like Brenda said, we looked like we were playing an intense game of Twister because we were literally knotted in a ball. Arms, legs, torsos, and heads were all over the place, and I swore that someone must've hit me so hard in the 'nads that my dick now poked out between my butt cheeks.

Well, at least everyone was back and safe. And in one tangled piece.

"Oh, Christ, oh, Christ, oh, Christ..." Freddie groaned from somewhere southwest of my right knee. "I'll never be able to breed ever."

"I'm so glad I'm wearing jeans, not a dress," Wade stammered, her voice a bit muffled. I guessed that she was unlucky enough to be buried under a pile of boys who were bigger than her. "Or I'd be tearing the balls off whoever's got his appendage jammed against my girl parts."

"I can't feel my foot." That was Ridley, who sounded like he was on top somewhere.

"Eek! Stop! Stop! Oh, my God, that was *so* wrong!" Wade yelped.

"Sorry! Sorry! I couldn't feel my foot! I didn't know where it was! I'm sorry! Please don't tell my parents I accidentally sexually harassed you!"

"Let me say that it's going to be a real bitch trying to get ourselves untangled," Peter said, his voice tight, from somewhere northwest of my left kidney. "We'd better hurry. I'm upside-down, and certain body parts are starting to shrivel from lack of blood."

"Get used to it," I said. It occurred to me then that I was literally lying on my right cheek, and I had no idea what the rest of my body looked like. "I live with that every day."

"Oh, lord, Althea, are you videotaping them yet?" Brenda asked.

"Yep. It's a keeper. I just need to use the right kind of background music for it when I edit the hell out of it and post it online."

Bitch.

* * * *

The next hour or so was spent with us being examined closely, one by one, with Dr. Dibbs all serious and official, while Brenda seemed to be struggling to wipe this shit-eating grin off her face. I made sure to glare at her when it was my turn to be looked over for physical damage, infections, and mental instability.

"You're mocking our pain," I said. "We could've all been stuck in that stupid-ass game."

"Oh, I'm so glad that you're all back, for sure," she said without skipping a beat while turning my bared right arm to find cuts and bruises. "I just can't get that image of the superheroes all lying in a literal ball against the wall."

I narrowed my eyes at her when she moved to my left arm and then ordered me to lift my shirt, so she could check my front and back. "Be glad that you've got Althea's pictures and video as keepsakes. You can watch that video again and again if you want to relive the moment."

"Oh, I plan to, hon. No worries there." Then she stood up, pinched my cheek, and then ruffled my hair. "You're fine. Just a few light bruises on your back. Good job."

A few aspirin pills later, we were once again sitting on the floor of my "classroom," and I made sure to give Wade my chair and desk since it looked like we destroyed the ones she used earlier because they were standing in our way when we tumbled back into the real world, a knotted ball of humanity. Dr. Dibbs, Althea, and Brenda all briefed us about what happened, but we pretty much knew what was going on outside, thanks to Althea's frequent communications. We found out that we had about four minutes left to spare, and that Althea's efforts at trying to punch her way through the game as well as possess the characters in order to communicate brought out new "adjunct powers" according to Dr. Dibbs, which she should be able to develop even more during the heroes' practice rescue missions. I'd no idea what "adjunct powers" meant, but seeing as how I wasn't a hero, I figured that I shouldn't care.

That hacker guy—O'Keefe (if that was his real name)—was good in what he did, but he was nowhere near Arachnaman's level when it came to super villainy.

"I wonder what he meant when he said that his mind-reading powers were accidental," I said. "I mean, sure, he was able to have that mental link with his brother, and that was how he learned how to mess around with a game, but 'accidental'?"

Everyone shrugged and shook their heads.

"It seems like a very minor power," Brenda said as she leaned across a wall, studying us. "Maybe he was a genetic experiment that was only partially successful? Or it wasn't even meant to happen?"

"It's possible. Kind of creepy thinking along those lines, but considering how things have turned out for Vintage City because of those geneticists, I wouldn't be surprised if someone might've messed around when he wasn't supposed to and only managed to partially manipulate this kid's DNA," Peter replied. "We might never know, now that he's disappeared."

"I wonder now if he'll come back and work with Arachnaman." Wade swept her gaze across the room. "My gut tells me that he won't. Like, his powers were only good for this one shot at getting back at us. They've probably weak-ened because of it, or they might deteriorate. I have a feeling that if Arachna-man comes back, it'll just be him. He's already way too smart and good at what he does to depend on little brother for extra help."

Everyone murmured either their agreement or their doubts. Althea was set to hack into Renaissance High's database to see if she could find something on O'Keefe, though she was convinced that he'd have erased his tracks pretty darned well by now.

As for Trini and Dario, who weren't there...

"I'm afraid we had to purge their memories," Dr. Dibbs said as he sat at his desk like he always did when I had "school" there. "But don't worry. The process is very safe, and we didn't have to use it on full blast, so to speak. Their knowl-edge of your true identities only happened in a matter of an hour, probably a little more, and that includes briefing time here as well as the actual game-play-ing. It didn't take much for us to erase that moment in their lives."

"I hope there aren't any side effects," I said dourly.

"No, there aren't. Just a sudden desire to take a nap, which I believe they ended up doing after we dropped them off near their home. A bit of hypnotism worked into the program to enable them to function automatically from the moment we erased their memories to the moment when they walked through their front door." Dr. Dibbs spread his hands out in front of him. "They go in-side, greet the family, and go upstairs to sleep. When they wake up, they'll re-member nothing but their time spent window-shopping downtown, which was where Miss Althea found them."

We all turned to Althea. How did she know they were out? Did she start reading minds as well? She shrugged. "Spur of the moment stuff—I knew Trini loves playing video games, so I texted her by worming my way into her phone to see if she could help us out. Those things are so easy to possess, especially when I'm hooked up to a bunch of laptops."

I shook my head. I guess it was all good if neither of them could remember my Majorly Embarrassing Nerd Moment ™ with those knives. As far as Althea went, I suppose I was better off not making any references to my Legolas fight-ing methods and humiliate myself by reminding her about it. "Man, this is nuts. And let me tell you, I'm swearing off computer games. Except for Pac-Man and

Tetris. Those I can do and not freak out over because of post-traumatic stress syndrome."

"Yeah," Freddie piped up, rubbing the back of his neck. "That was way too close for comfort. And you know, sitting alone in that damn banquet room, not able to talk or move while surrounded by dead people? That really sucked ass."

"I wanted to burn the whole freakin' castle down," Wade said, making a face. "It was nasty."

Peter shrugged, smiling sheepishly. "I was lucky enough to be able to move even though I was still confined. I tried to stay above those bodies while I waited and avoid looking at them."

A few more minutes followed, during which we started talking all together, sort of like a moment of depressurizing. Brenda, Dr. Dibbs, and Althea consulted with each other—most likely regarding Renaissance High's database and maybe other things as far as tracking O'Keefe down was concerned. Still, that stunt of his wasn't considered as threatening as any attacks aimed at Vintage City overall, though I would've argued against that. Vintage could've lost its superheroes save for Magnifiman and Spirit Wire. All the same, I kept my mouth shut, thanked the cosmos that the ordeal was over, and then demanded pizza.

"Oh, yeah." Ridley scrambled to his feet, brushed off his clothes, and trotted off to make the phone call.

In the meantime, people moved around to stretch sore muscles and raid Brenda's back room for something to drink. I stayed behind, gingerly rubbing my back. Then I felt a gentle tap between my shoulders and found Peter standing behind me, giving me a silly grin.

"Good job back there, by the way," he said. "I saw what you tried to do, helping Wade like that when she was starting to fade. That was mighty honorable of you, Eric Plath."

I blinked. "It was? That's what you call it? Huh—I've never been called that before. Usually I'm a whiner or a drama queen."

"Well, those, too, but you're still ace in my book." He leaned close and kissed me. And, shocker of all shockers, I didn't grab him by the collar and yank him back when he pulled away, so he could give me a thorough tonsil job. I thought that a quick kiss on the mouth was plenty sweet.

I guess I must've hit my head harder than I thought.

"I'm sorry I got everyone in this mess," I said, drooping a little when it hit me. "All I wanted was to come up with a birthday gift for you that'd be something you've never seen before. I didn't expect to get us all sucked into the game because of some psycho's brotherly love thing, which, by the way, is creepy as hell." I shrugged when Peter's brows went up. "I mean, you know—you've got everything you need or want. Can't really top that, can I?"

Peter smiled and tweaked my nose lightly. "You already have. In fact, you always do. I've never had anyone go through all this trouble just for a birthday gift, Eric. I hope you know how much that means to me." When I said nothing because my face was burning and I was in danger of toeing the ground and going, "Aw, shucks, it ain't nuthin,'" Peter chuckled, flicked my bangs off my face, and said, "Now let's go get some pizza, you big sap. All the power used up in the game drained me of everything I ate since I was born."

If I was the big sap, what would *he* be, the sugary bastard? Well, whatever—he still got me all icky-giddy and stuff with all that sweet talk.

We were alone in the room at that point, and I could hear everyone else yakking in the main customer area. Peter and I took our time walking out, arms resting around each others' waists, while we talked about stuff.

"I really hope Trini and Dario aren't going to be messed up by the memory zapper thingie," I said. "And what would happen if their memories turned out to be repressed, not erased, and they start remembering things down the line? What then?"

"I wouldn't worry about it. The Sentries know what they're doing. You've seen them fix everything before, right? Like, turn those human arachnids back or the toddlers—and both of us! And we're all safe and healthy."

"Yeah, I know, but I can't help but feel bad, anyway. They got dragged into the whole mess because of me."

Peter suddenly stopped just shy of the door. He leaned close and whispered, "If I get all frisky with you after this, will you promise not to get all guilt-trippy over something you shouldn't even sweat over?"

"I'm easily bought," I said, snapping to attention. "I totally come cheap."

Peter led me out into the main customer area, where everyone was killing time waiting for the pizza delivery guy to show up. "Atta boy. I knew you were special."

* * * *

Ridley made good his promise to me, which pretty much solidified his status as my newest and greatest BFF. He ordered four pizzas, not two, and we all barreled back into my "classroom" with the loot, Wade and Althea bringing up the rear with the bottles of soda and paper cups (recyclable, by the way).

The next hour was nothing but a disgusting scene of teenage gluttony, with the girls on par with the boys in levels of greed. Dr. Dibbs took his share, and so did Brenda, who had to eat hers in her back room because her shop was still open, while Dr. Dibbs also set up camp with her there, so he could hammer away at his laptop and not be bothered by thick, intimidating clouds of adolescence. Not sure if he was going to find anything on O'Keefe, but it also wouldn't be a surprise if he was as bored as everyone else because of the current lull in crime, and he was surfing the 'net. Hopefully not looking for porn because I really, *really* didn't need a mental picture of Dr. Dibbs and naked action stuck in my head. After the trauma of having to see corpses, skeletons, and zombies up close, I didn't need another one of those.

"Hey, to Ridley and Eric!" Wade cried, raising a cup of soda up for a toast. She sat on the floor, her back against the wall, and her lap cradling a paper plate that looked like it was about to dissolve under all that grease from the tower of pizza slices she'd hoarded. "They're the real heroes of this adventure!"

"Yo, Ridley! Eric!" Freddie chimed in, raising his cup. "You guys rocked, man! By the way, Eric, thanks for wearing me. I thought I was going to be carried by someone, considering, you know, how cheesy my new form was. I could've been happy waiting around as a unicorn or a dwarf. Whatever works well in a fairy tale, anyway."

I narrowed my eyes at him. "That'd have to be your gayest moment yet, dude. And that's as far as you'll ever get with me."

"Oh, come on, you looked great in armor!"

"Nice try, perv. You were damned heavy."

"If it's any comfort, Eric, Freddie could've turned into a full suit of armor, which includes a codpiece," Wade piped up. When I stared at her, she added, "You're welcome." That girl had no shame, I swear.

Ridley grinned, shrugged, and turned beet-red. I think he stayed beet-red the whole time we ate, which made me wonder at one point if we should call an ambulance because that color looked unhealthy. But that was Ridley for you. I hoped he enjoyed the attention because he sure deserved it.

We cleaned up and helped dispose of the boxes and paper cups and plates. Leftover slices of pizza were stuffed in large food storage bags—though as to why Brenda kept, like, a gazillion boxes of those in her back room was a mystery—and then distributed among everyone. Brenda and Dr. Dibbs refused, so we all went our separate ways, each a plastic storage bag filled with leftover pizza slices richer.

Oh, and Peter made good his promise. See, there was a reason why I fell in love with him.

"You know, I started off hating all this peace and quiet around here, but now I'm kind of glad that we got this quick breather from crime-fighting," I said, grinning up at him and blinking away the haze.

As always, we were both cramped in the back seat of his little sports car. Not like we had much choice, really, with our families home and so on. And thank heavens for quiet country roads with tons of trees and helpful super big rocks outside Vintage. Okay, make that boulders that worked well as shields.

He hovered above me, looking as glassy-eyed as I was. "Huh?"

"I enjoyed our time together. I mean, not just you and me, but with the others, you know? It's—it's kind of weird, but nice."

Peter laughed quietly. Man, he was hot when laughed quietly. Especially when he was still a bit flushed from the first round. "Weird but nice?" Oh, and halfway incoherent, too. He made speech issues totally hot.

"It feels like being in a regular social group, which I guess we are, but I know I'm the only guy in Vintage City who's best buddies with superheroes." I somehow managed to free up my numbed arm and reach up to touch his cheek. "I like seeing you guys behaving like regular kids. It was crazy fun—okay, dangerous with that video game bit, but crazy fun. Hopefully you'll get more chances like this."

"Mmm—I have a feeling that it might be another while before we get that chance."

"In that case, I guess I might as well take full advantage of this as much as I can." I pulled him down for another round because, you know, the recovery time for a sixteen-year-old boy was just mind-boggling.

Chapter 13

Sure enough, the next day, a couple of incidents (unrelated, apparently) involving bored housewives stuffing their massive purses with unpaid merchandise and then getting busted became Vintage City's Breaking News of the Day. I guess that'd be one step up from scraping the bottom of the barrel, but at least criminals—or criminal wannabes—were finally crawling out of the woodwork.

Of course, there was also that chance those shoplifting housewives were so bored with Vintage being eerily crime-free for a while that they decided to shake things up a bit. Just like those missing persons—looked like there were a couple more since I was last told about them—they probably ran away from Vintage City to escape their mind-numbing boredom. The only person who got something good out of this was Bambi Bailey, though it was clear that she was struggling hard to keep herself from yawning so much in front of the camera.

At any rate, I'd gotten so used to this break from mayhem that I went back to hitting my head against my bedroom wall over Peter's birthday gift. Eventually I decided to stop giving myself an ulcer over it. I'd earned some money, anyway. I could always take him out and let him decide what he wanted to do—beyond playing my favorite game of Sweaty, Sticky Human Pretzel ™ in the back seat of his car.

In the meantime, life droned on in the Plath household, the upside being Mom's defenses finally crumbling where Grimm was concerned.

"Your father uses Grimm for post-work therapy from 5:30 to 6:30 on the weekdays," she said over breakfast on Monday. "I'm taking the 7:30 to 8:30 time slot, and when I say that's sacred, I mean it."

"Gotcha, Mom," Liz said, blinking, before turning to look at me from across the table and silently mouthing, "WTF?"

I shrugged and ate my breakfast, occasionally turning around to check up on my cat and see if he needed more food. Grimm seemed busy in the corner of the kitchen, scarfing up his canned food. Then a thought hit me, and I frowned.

"Hey, wait a second," I muttered, turning to stare at my eggs as I mulled things over. "Grimm's technically my cat, and people are hogging him for therapy."

"Eric, you're not charging us fees to use your cat for blood pressure relief," Mom said, her voice cutting straight through the thick soup of ideas that swirled in my brain. When I looked at her, shocked, she added, "I can see that devious little mind of yours at work, mister. You don't even need to say anything." She took a sip of her coffee.

"What the—how would you know what I'm thinking?" I asked, all outraged. Kind of, anyway. I mean, she was right, but I still thought to look as appalled as I possibly could.

"I'm your mother, and you inherited your grandfather's penchant for deviance. He wasn't kicked out of school for nothing, you know. Now finish your breakfast and hustle on down to school. Grimm will be fine looking after the house for us."

Well, so much for earning some extra money for college. I would've said that, but with Mom getting caffeinated, it was best to let things slide. For now, that is. I wasn't done yet with the free therapy that my cat was being forced to give. It'd be like having Grimm work in some seedy sweatshop and threatened with deportation if he didn't do his job.

When I got to "school," Brenda met me with cookies, tea, and some news. "So it looks like O'Keefe wasn't O'Keefe, but that shouldn't come as a surprise, and his trail's grown cold, though for good reason."

"I expected that," I said, munching thoughtfully. "But shouldn't the Sentries be interviewing Arachnaman for more information?"

"They did, yeah. Yesterday, in fact, thanks to that handy-dandy truth serum we injected him with. That 'accidental' mind-reading power the kid claimed to have? That wasn't someone in the genetics lab doing something under the table. It was Arachnaman himself, experimenting on a random kid he met before his attacks on Vintage. He doesn't have a brother."

I stared at her. "What the what?"

"The kid was a runaway. He was homeless." Brenda paused to refill her teacup. "Arachnaman found him somewhere, lured him with drugs, and injected O'Keefe with what he called 'brain probes' that lay dormant till the moment Arachnaman activated them himself."

That sounded like what the Devil's Trill did to me once upon a time. I shook my head. "It's pretty hard wrapping my head around that. Then again, considering everything that's happened since the heroes and villains came into their powers, I really shouldn't be questioning anything. I mean, this sounds kinda *Star Trek*-y, know what I mean?"

"I know. But with these supervillains, I wouldn't bat an eyelash. They're all brilliant in their own ways. I mean, think about the Debutantes—I'm sure their Über Metamorphier shocked the hell out of you, right?" Brenda grinned when she saw the look on my face.

"I had to pinch myself when I saw that contraption. I've always thought they were just a couple of dumb, high maintenance bullies, but their recent attack on Vintage City was brilliant work. It definitely required way more brain cells than I thought they have."

At this moment Dr. Dibbs poked his head out from the corner of the hallway that led to the shop's back rooms, and he waved and then disappeared. That was sort of like my warning bell in school. The second warning would be Dr. Dibbs hollering for me to get my ass in the "classroom" before he filled out a detention slip. So I stuffed my face with another cookie, chewed it up at the speed of light, and then swallowed, ignoring the look of morbid fascination on Brenda's face as she watched me.

"Yeah, anyway," she said, taking a sip of her tea, "you shouldn't underestimate these guys. Arachnaman, I think, would be the smartest and most creative of the bunch, and maybe it's his bigotry that feeds his genius in some perverse way. But he's the most dangerous of the group. And as for O'Keefe, he's gone, probably ran off to another city, and according to his so-called mentor, he wouldn't remember a damned thing about what happened here."

"The brain probes had an expiration date?"

She shrugged. "It looks like it. They were only needed to hunt down the heroes and make them play into a trap that O'Keefe put together under Arachnaman's directions via that temporary mental link they both had. Once the trap was delivered to the heroes, O'Keefe's time as Arachnaman's stooge was done, and he was free to go wherever he wanted to."

I finished my tea and hopped off my chair. "I'll bet you, though, if Arachnaman himself was the one who set up that trap from scratch, it would've been way harder to crack it."

"I wouldn't bet against that. Now go on and shock the world with your schoolboy skills." That was a nice send-off, I suppose, though to this day, I still can't figure out if Brenda was being sarcastic or not.

* * * *

Peter picked me up after "school." It was technically a shocker, but at that point, living in Vintage City had gone far in its daily "Why Life Here Shouldn't Shock You" lessons, so I was more like pleasantly surprised to find him waiting for me in the customer area.

"We're meeting Trini and Dario at Dog-in-a-Bun in about twenty minutes," he said after the usual meet-and-greet (read: virginal hug and peck on the mouth because Brenda was making faces at us from the safety of her counter). "The GSA scheme's coming along. We got the backing of the student body president, at least, and we're trying to schmooze with Mrs. Klein about being a faculty moderator."

We strolled down the main avenue toward our default hot dog place. Here and there, we'd stop to window shop or to point something out in the landscape of Vintage City that made us laugh. I told Peter about adopting Grimm, and he ordered me to let him play with the cat whenever he visited.

"You'll have to put your name down on a schedule," I said. "If you want to use my cat for free therapy, you'll have to get in line. Grimm's schedule's pretty much filled up after office hours and after dinner." I paused, frowning, when another thought hit me. "By the way, I hope this doesn't mean that I'll be competing with my own pet for your attention."

Peter laughed and nudged me with his elbow, his hidden superpower almost sending me flying against a store's brick wall. Then he laughed again for forgetting his own strength and almost crushing my brains. I glared at him. Seriously, this whole unemployed superheroes thing was getting borderline creepy. I wondered how the others coped with all those hours of not seeing justice done. I wouldn't be surprised if they tore their homes apart, the same way dogs destroyed things when you don't take them out for daily walks or something.

Trini and Dario were already there when Peter and I arrived, and it was nice seeing Trini again. I couldn't help but think about the game and how she and her brother kicked major ass, helping me and Ridley whack our way to the castle, so we wouldn't lose any time. Dario was his sister's opposite in personality, though they were almost identical in physical characteristics save for their height. While Dario was clean-cut and almost pixie-ish with his short hair and big eyes, he was tall, while Trini was Wade-sized. He was also soft-spoken and easily embarrassed, almost nervous, judging from the way his eyes seemed to move constantly as though he were watching everyone around him. He also had a habit of slouching in his chair, like he wanted to shrink and disappear.

I figured it was because of his coming-out experience and how he likely felt uncomfortable being Dario and not a girl. I didn't know anything about transgender people because I never knew any till that moment, so I was at a loss as to how I could make Dario's experience a little easier. I figured I was probably better off not making a big deal out of it and just treating him no differently from everyone else.

I was also on full alert mode when we talked, looking out for signs of Trini or Dario's memory of the game. But nothing came out, even if it was just a slip of a tongue or a sudden weird look on their faces like when a moment of déjà vu or something happened. On one hand, I was relieved to know that my friends' superhero identities remained safe, but on the other, I still felt kind of bad that Trini and Dario were used like that, even though it was for a good purpose.

"You know, prom season's coming up," Trini said after a lull in the conversation. "If we don't have a GSA up and running by then, do you think it's possible for us to put together a GSA-type prom?"

Peter and I looked at each other. "I don't know, honestly," Peter said with a shrug. "I have a feeling that it'll end up being a private prom that's not sanctioned by the school."

"Well, do you think that people will give you a lot of grief if you two show up as prom dates?" Trini asked, nodding at us both, while Dario thoughtfully scraped excess chili off his hot dog.

"Good point, but wouldn't it be worth shaking things up by letting people know that gay kids go to the same school as them?" I answered. That was a brave thing to say, seeing as how I'd never done anything that overt since I came out. "I guess it'll boil down to what kind of support you guys get in the end. I don't know. Just wait and see?"

"Yeah, we'll have to deal with one thing at a time first. This is turning out to be bigger than I first expected, but we gotta start somewhere, right?" Trini grinned, blushing.

"And someone's gotta do it," Dario said, sinking in his seat another inch.

In a couple of minutes, we were all talking about stuff other than the GSA, but I couldn't help but look at Peter every once in a while and feel all proud of him for working with Trini on this. In fact, I was so proud that when he drove me home, I brought him upstairs and let him play with Grimm for as long as he wanted, while I put together some snacks downstairs.

Come to think of it, I was so damned proud that we ended up playing with the cat till my parents came home, and not once did I take advantage of our private time for five rounds of non-deflowering gay teen love sports. By the time Peter left, Grimm was so exhausted that he slept through his scheduled time with Dad and then Mom.

"What on earth did you kids do to this poor animal?" Dad asked, frowning at a limp and out cold Grimm, who lay draped in a boneless mass on his lap.

Mom didn't have much luck waking him, either. "Whatever organic herbs you give this cat, I want some of them," she said as she stared in amazement at the snoring mass of fur that wouldn't respond to her attention.

"It's called exercise, Mom," I said, beaming proudly like a real parent at the wreck of a cat she was trying hard to bond with. "I read online that good pet owners should spend as much time as they can playing with their dogs or cats."

"It looks more like being chased after by a freight train and not playing." Mom paused and gave Grimm a light poke with her finger. Nothing. In fact, Grimm almost slid off her lap, still passed out, and Mom had to catch him. "Okay, I guess I'll have to live vicariously through him sleeping like this." She continued stroking Grimm while changing the channels to her favorite evening crime drama.

Before I went to bed, I got online to see if there were any last minute cool things I could get for Peter even though I'd already convinced myself not to bother. And if I were to come away from that online surfing adventure with something substantial, it'd be the realization—or more like resigned acceptance—of how insane the 'net was. Like, one could start off with one thing in mind, do research along those lines, and then find himself going from one tangent to another till, by the time the hour was up, he'd have been exposed to about fifty million whacky things he never knew existed.

There was one site that caught my eye—a place that sold dolls that were similar to those super-expensive pretty boy dolls from Japan or Korea. But it was a local manufacturer, which I thought was really cool, and the dolls looked incredible—though maybe a bit spooky the way their eyes looked so real and the way they seemed to follow you when you moved, even though they were only images online. The dolls came in all kinds of costumes and hairstyles that one could mix and match and even customize. I checked out the prices and frowned. The dolls were way, way cheaper than those from Asia, if my memory served me right. At the same time, they also looked like they could be trendy—or something that people would go crazy over for a short amount of time until their novelty wore off. With a lower price compared to the original versions, I wouldn't be surprised if people had already started collections by now.

"Living Dolls," I muttered, reading out loud the dolls' basic description. "Well, I guess they're sort of like living dolls, the way they stare at you. Everything else is obviously fake. I mean, duh."

I read up some more on the dolls, clicking links here and there, and getting slightly creeped out by claims of "loyal companionship" or "fiercely close friendship" or even "protectors" of their owners. I grimaced. I felt myself growing more and more unsettled with every page I checked out.

I found, though, that I had a hard time leaving the site. There was something attractive about those dolls even though they weren't my type, so I bookmarked the page before checking my email and then shutting my computer down. When I went to bed, I kept looking over my shoulder even though I knew I was alone save for Grimm. Maybe it was an effect of the experiences I had being trapped in a horror computer game, but strangely I somehow felt like there was someone else there with me. Which, of course, made me wonder all the more if I owned one of those dolls, like, would it make me feel like it was alive or something? That was what their website made me think, anyway.

"Meh. So dumb," I said, yawning, as I tucked Grimm under the covers and listened to his purring till it finally faded, and I fell asleep immediately after.

* * * *

Peter's birthday finally arrived after a few more days of humdrum existence in Vintage City. He celebrated with his family first and then the superheroes the next day. His family's celebration was quiet and private, he said. They took him to a swanky restaurant, naturally, and showered him with high-end gifts.

As far as what the heroes did for him, I never got to find out beforehand, but I didn't care at that point, having suffered through the agony of planning and stuff. They were more than welcome to do whatever they wanted, even if it meant hosting a surprise birthday for Peter that was superhero-themed and seriously, seriously cheesy. They could always give me the scoop after the fact; for my part, I was too busy focusing on how best to pamper him even more. The whole time I lay low, of course, and let him enjoy being spoiled by everyone, and didn't care if I had to wait one more day to celebrate it with him.

An idea finally clicked in the meantime, and I went to the library to see how possible it was. Then I went to the store to buy some stuff for his birthday meal.

The only bummer was that our day fell on a Thursday, so we spent most of it in school first and then afterward enjoying a quiet, warm time in the same little park-like place where I first saw Grimm. I'd put together a picnic basket with Brenda's help—even waking up super early to haul off Mom's old picnic basket packed with raw materials that I got from the store (okay, so Dad drove me to the antique shop)—and then tuck away his gift.

"You really shouldn't have," he said, grinning and coloring, when I gave him the package. "Thank you."

"You can thank me properly after we're done eating," I replied, and ordered him to open it up while I pulled out sandwiches, a bag of chips, and sodas. I even brought some of the leftover recyclable paper cups from our pizza party days ago because, you know, one didn't have a proper picnic without glasses, plates, silverware, and napkins—even if they were all paper or plastic. He chirped and did what he was told.

"Whoa."

I glanced up to find him staring at the cover of one book first before turning it over, running his fingers slowly over the tattered and discolored leather. Then he opened it and pored through about a dozen pages before finally looking up at me, eyes wide. The second book sat on the table, waiting to be explored. It was just as old and fancy-looking as the first one, and I liked the way it smelled. You know, like an old book.

"Where did you get these?" he asked. He sounded almost awed.

"At the library's store—where they sell their old stuff." I squelched my excitement. "Do you like it? I mean, them. You've got one more to check out, by the way." I nodded at the other book that he hadn't examined yet.

I watched his grin broaden till it practically broke his face. "Eric, this is fantastic! It looks like the first edition of this book! Thank you!"

He slid off his bench, hurried over to me, and gave me a big, long, wet one on the mouth. In public. In broad daylight. I stared at him, wide-eyed, at first when he pulled away and then walked back to his bench. At that point, I didn't give a rat's ass if anyone anywhere saw us. All that mattered was watching Peter rediscover his old passion for poetry in that old book of World War I sonnets from his favorite British poets as well as poets he'd never read about before. The second book I bought him was also the first edition of a collection of biographies of some of those poets. I decided to get it because I figured that those books together would help Peter's appreciation of World War I poetry deepen even more. I didn't know anyone else our age who read that stuff, and in a way, I felt damned proud of being the boyfriend of a rare breed of teenager.

"If there's anything I learned from your birthday, it's to keep things simple and go back to the basics," I said. When he glanced up and looked at me, I shrugged, adding, "Like I said before, these breaks from crime-fighting are so rare, and it's great seeing you and the others do what regular teenagers do. I'm just taking advantage of whatever's left of your down time." When he didn't say anything, I felt myself blush. "I like seeing you smile a lot and not be so tired every time. I know, it sounds kind of sappy."

Peter's grin softened. "I love you, but you already know that."

"Yeah, but hearing that never gets old. Love you, too. And happy birthday."

Peter looked down at the book he held, looking so giddy all over again. "This is so cool," he muttered.

I laughed quietly the whole time I prepared our picnic because Peter suddenly forgot about me as he started reading the biographies first, the look of wonder and bliss on his face something that was so rare in an overworked teenage superhero that I plain didn't have the heart to bother him. Too bad I didn't have a camera with me then; on the other hand, this was a moment worth keeping in memory, not in pixels. So I sat there, waiting for him to stop on his own time, resting my chin on my hand as I watched, still laughing to myself.

Don't miss out!

Visit the website below and you can sign up to receive emails whenever Hayden Thorne publishes a new book. There's no charge and no obligation.

https://books2read.com/r/B-A-LFQC-BNFRB

BOOKS 2 READ

Connecting independent readers to independent writers.

About the Author

I've lived most of my life in the San Francisco Bay Area though I wasn't born there (or, indeed, the USA). I'm married with no kids and three cats.

I started off as a writer of gay young adult fiction, specializing in contemporary fantasy, historical fantasy, and historical genres. My books ranged from a superhero fantasy series to reworked and original folktales to Victorian ghost fiction.

I've since expanded to gay New Adult fiction, which reflects similar themes as my YA books and varies considerably in terms of romantic and sexual content.

While I've published with a small press in the past, I now self-publish my books. Please visit my site for exclusive sales and publishing updates.

Read more at https://haydenthorne.com.

www.ingramcontent.com/pod-product-compliance
Lightning Source LLC
Chambersburg PA
CBHW021450150726
47989CB00001B/480